D0537830

THE BrODSKY TOUCH

BY THE SAME AUTHOR

Sucker
Spilt Milk
Transit
The Honey Trap

THE BRODSKY TOUCH

Lana Citron

BLOOMSBURY

First published in Great Britain 2007

Copyright © 2007 by Lana Citron

The moral right of the author has been asserted

No part of this book may be used or reproduced in any manner
whatsoever without written permission from the Publisher except in the
case of brief quotations embodied in critical articles or reviews

Bloomsbury Publishing Plc, 36 Soho Square, London W1D 3QY

A CIP catalogue record for this book is available from the British Library

ISBN 978 0 7475 8042 3

10 9 8 7 6 5 4 3 2 1

Typeset by Hewer Text UK Ltd, Edinburgh
Printed in Great Britain by Clays Ltd, St Ives plc

Bloomsbury Publishing, London, New York and Berlin

All papers used by Bloomsbury Publishing are natural,
recyclable products made from wood grown in well-managed
forests. The manufacturing processes conform to the
environmental regulations of the country of origin

www.bloomsbury.com

The Brodsky Touch
n. when everything one touches turns to
shit; opposite of Midas Touch

'THANK YOU . . . AND GOOD NIGHT'

There came an ungodly roar from the crowd – a roar of appreciation, I hasten to add. I did my best to milk it; I bowed, curtsied, punched the air and, most importantly, didn't wake up. This wasn't a dream. My eyelids weren't about to ease open, contented with the night's illusory whim of fancy. No, this was 100 per cent unadulterated reality and I believed that this evening would mark the beginning of a new era for me. I was sweating profusely, as adrenalin was flooding my body. It was all reminiscent of when I lost my virginity, only this time I reached a climax. My eyes scanned the audience. There were about thirty people present, which was fair enough, considering it was a wet Monday night in a room above a grotty goth pub in Camden Town, London.

The occasion was the quarter-finals of the 'Women Can Be Funny Too' competition. I had made it through three previous rounds, yes, *thrice* had I proved myself and, judging by tonight's performance, it was an immodest certainty that I would go on to the semi-finals and then the finals. From there I'd be catapulted from my normal, north London, 'spod-u-like' existence up to the city of Edinburgh, Land of the

Scots, where I would reside for the entire month of August and partake in a stand-up show at the grand Edinburgh Fringe Festival. Of course, this would represent a mere stepping stone, for I would then be hurled heavenward. Make no mistake, I was starbound, next stop Hollywood. I was going to hang with Madonna, sing with André 3000 and make love to the A-listers. See, *this* was my dream and the reason I'd been working my ass off for the past year or, in truth, even longer.

Ever since I was a little girl I'd wanted fame. Not in a D-list, celebrity, must-expose-my-breasts sort of way (especially not since giving birth). Nor was it the trappings of a luxury lifestyle I was after, though I knew I would come to appreciate it. It was more of a deep desire – indeed, I would go even further: it was a need, a subterranean guttural ache to express myself on a global scale. Being a shortarse, modelling was out of the question, although I wouldn't have turned down a midget catalogue. Sure, I toyed with other artistic vocations: acting, painting, singing, ballet, operatic diva, rock chick, gangster moll, weather girl, but was continually put off by the number of qualifications required. Then, thumbing my way through the pages of *Floodlight*, I chanced upon a 'How to be a comedian in nine easy steps' course and promptly signed up. It required neither a CV nor previous experience, simply a cheque. Hurrah! I qualified. I enrolled, studied hard, learned how to create a joke, shape a joke, tell a joke. Laughter is more than a muscular contraction, my friend (although that is exactly what it is). Anyway, the art of evoking laughter captivated me and, following my comedic graduation, I began to gig, gradually and painstakingly learning the craft of the comic. Nine months later, the time was ripe, the moment within my grasp and I was dropping punchlines, well . . . like a mother.

Yes, finally the smell of success flirted with my nostrils, which flared open to inhale all the more. Agh . . . if only I could freeze-frame that moment, for the audience continued to clap as I continued to bow, prolonging it further by pointing down to the invisible orchestra, upward to the unknown gods, finally acknowledging my co-competitors (who all looked unreservedly nervous) before Fat Adrian the MC bounced onstage, grabbed my free fist and yanked it upwards.

'Ladies and gentlemen,' he cried, 'let's give it up one last time for the one, the only, a close, personal, showbiz friend of mine, little Issy Brodsky.'

Me: Issy Brodsky.
Age: thirty-recurring.
Physique: normally size ten, though being on stage is similar to telly, it puts on at least half a stone; as for the other half, let's just say I enjoy my food.
Ego: rising.
Status: mainly confused, single mother to one child, a boy of five years old.
Love interest: die-hard romantic and girlfriend to Scarface.

3

Relationship at present: rocky.

Job: hanging on by the skin of my teeth.

Position: in glamorous terminology, 'agent provocateur'; in vernacular, two-bit private detective.

Financial ranking: Red alert, red alert . . .

Jubilantly, I pushed my way through the thirty-strong throng towards a table of loyal supporters on the far side of the room, otherwise known as my work colleagues. The entire Honey Trap Undercover Detective Agency was conspicuously out in full force.

'Nice one, Brodsky,' yelled Nads.

Though Nadia was younger and far more aesthetically pleasing than yours truly, I didn't hold it against her (for long) and considered her a true friend, a best friend and, besides, she'd always laughed at my jokes – a habit established way before I went on the comedy course. Nadia was someone I could rely on to give me an honest appraisal of my performance.

'Nads, did you notice how nervous I was at the beginning of my set?' I whispered.

'You mean the shaky voice?'

'Yeah . . .'

'I thought it was on purpose.'

'Phew. And what about when I dropped the mic?'

'Issy, you were fantastic,' Maria cried. Maria, co-worker and chief babysitter extraordinaire, flung herself upon me. 'Very brave.'

'You're just saying that . . .'

'No, I mean it,' and she repeated earnestly, 'very

brave.' Tears of pride glistened at the edges of her eyes as she grasped me to her mammoth chest.

A swift, sharp whack to my spine released me from the quicksands of Maria's flesh. I jerked backwards like a Wellington boot being yanked from a pool of mud. It was Trisha, second-in-command of the Honey Trap. She was a woman of much military bearing, and slightly suspicious of me. Put it this way: when I stepped out of line, she was sure to catch me.

'Got to hand it to you, Issy, you've really come on in the past year. Miles better than your first gig,' Trisha observed.

'Don't remind me . . .'

I cringed at the memory. It had been a truly woeful event.

'You may have found your vocation.' Trisha raised a glass to me.

Naturally, I reached out to take it. Unfortunately, it wasn't an offer – it was hers. My mild embarrassment amplified when Fiona blared out, for all and sundry to hear: 'Brodsky, thought the drinks were on you to-night. Mine's a vodka tonic.'

Fiona was my top boss, Honey founder and one of Europe's leading experts on all things 'Trappable' (ie potentially erring partners). Having once been a man, she knew the male psyche well, but had acquired the capacity to be a complete bitch as soon as she'd gone for the full chop.

Okay, confession time: I had had to bribe most of my colleagues to guarantee their presence/support.

'Fiona,' I muttered, 'I strictly stipulated only the first two.'

'I jest, Brodsky,' she smiled. 'You did good. Well done.'

I beamed, chuffed to bits that the force were all present to witness my glorious ascension to the very first rung of superstardom.

'A word in your ear, Brodsky,' Fiona murmured.

I hated it when she said stuff like that, suspecting she'd discovered something was amiss, usually that which I should have done, did do, or forgot to do. Like when I mixed up two assignments, mistaking one client's husband for another, leading to false accusations, recriminations and, ultimately, two marriages dissolved. Puff, one, two, three, and like a stack of cards they crumpled. Or then there was the time I accidentally got involved with a client – physically involved, the full ding-dong, beep-beep, toot-toot (I kid you not), and committed the cardinal sin of Honey Trapping. Agh, fool that I was to allow such a transgression to occur. The forbidden line crossed. For one can flirt, tease, toy with, trifle with, importune even, but never ever, on pain of P45-dom, ever, ever, ever, ever, ever, on no account whatsoever (ever), have full and complete carnal knowledge of any of the clients.

Yeah, I lost my job over that and, though reinstated (it's a long story and a riveting read, in a book called *The Honey Trap* – go figure – go buy), I have been on a prolonged probation ever since. One false move and I'm history. It's much like living under threat of an ever-increasing congestion zone that will eventually incorporate the whole of London within the M25. Don't get me wrong, I do hate my job and can't wait until I'm ready to make the all important step to professional comedian, ie, one that is paid, but as reality decrees and everyone acknowledges, it is incredibly difficult for most nannyless/grannyless mothers of young kids to find a job complementing school hours and term times, never mind securing one that is somewhat fulfilling, challenging and well paid. Being a lone parent, Honey Trapping had turned out to be the perfect solution. Pre hooking up with my boyfriend, Scarface, it meant I had, by default at least, a semblance of a social life.

'That woman there . . .' Fiona pointed to the side of the stage where a tall, thin, spiky-looking woman was deliberating with her more dumpy, pasty-faced counterpart. Both women were judges of the night's competition and both were high profile in the world of female comedy. The podglet was Nell Tony, one of the top agents in London. If one was lucky enough to get on Nell's books, a TV job was almost guaranteed. The other woman was Geraldine McIntosh, the hard-core promoter, and the one to impress at my level of the game. Without her putting a good word in, gigs were very hard to come by. She had the ability to showcase talent and, if she liked what she saw, you could bypass several years of hard slog and fast-forward to a ten-minute slot in a stand-up comedy show at the Edinburgh Festival. Hence . . .

'That's Geraldine. Geraldine McIntosh, she's one of the judges.'

Geraldine must have felt our eyes on her, for at that very instant she looked up and across at me. I smiled in a 'pick me' fashion, which she returned in a non-committal way.

'Geraldine . . . Gerry . . .' Fiona was off on one.

'Do you know her?' I asked.

'Know her,' Fiona repeated, her gaze firmly fixed on the subject, whose own was firmly fixed on Fiona's. It was anyone's guess who'd blink first. Geraldine lost. Her lids flickered, then opened and closed in what could only be labelled as utter bafflement. Her eyes then narrowed, her brows met, her forehead scrunched, while Fiona, wearing a mischievous grin, daintily waved across at her.

'Old school friend, Brodsky,' Fiona whispered to me. 'Let's see if she can work it out.'

A double-take was trebled, then quadrupled and eventually Geraldine's jaw unhinged and dropped open.

'Oh my . . . I don't . . . I can't . . .' and she strode towards us.

'Bingo,' smiled Fiona, throwing her arms warmly around her. 'Geraldine McIntosh.'

'Duncan! What happened to you?'

'The Full Monty,' I quipped. 'The super-chop,' I winked, my elbow nudging upwards. 'The no-going-back, full-gender makeover . . .' I was on a roll of metaphors, making the most of my Geraldine McIntosh first face-to-face.

She completely blanked me, her expression one of stupefied amazement.

'Duncan! You . . . you . . .'

'Fiona,' Fiona reintroduced herself.

They stood eyeballing each other like besotted teens.

'It must be, what, thirty years?' Fiona gasped.

'At least,' Geraldine sighed.

'I can't believe it. After all this time,' Fiona half-whispered, the edges of her eyes moistening.

Feeling like Fiona's cast-off (a spare prick), I finally got the hint. 'Anyone want a drink?' As there were no forthcoming replies, I left them to it and went looking for Scarface, my boyfriend.

Scarface and I were originally drawn together through hatred. At first glance he was, to me, an arrogant, self-centred, younger man and I, to him, a frazzled, frustrated single mum who'd put a jinx on him after he complained about my son Max making too much noise.

See, one night while changing a bulb he fell off a ladder and that was how he'd acquired his scar, nickname and near electrocuted himself in the process. The poor guy was hospitalised and I blamed myself when it happened. How stereotypically female of me, especially considering we weren't even going out at that stage. Nevertheless, over time we slowly warmed to one another. Mere acknowledgements turned to 'Hi's, which turned to minor conversations. Then, on the night of my first ever stand-up gig, he walked me home, which I considered gentlemanly, notwithstanding the fact that he lived directly above me. We stalled outside my door and he kissed me with such intensity I was suctioned to him like a mollusc.

And before I knew it, I was in a state of conjugation. I was conjugating him.

I him
You me
Me you
He me
She he
We us

Yes, I regressed to the state of a love-obsessed teenager.

How pathetic yet unsurprising. For the next three months a full orchestra followed me around – metaphorically, you understand. Singing birds appeared from every nook and cranny, chirruping and twittering like there was no delineation between dusk and dawn. People smiled at me inanely as I walked down the street. God damn it, friggin' kiddies ran up just to touch the hemline of my skirt. I was a flower, my petals unfurling and was being touched in places that hadn't been touched in a long time. (Pervert, but let's not go there – oh, okay then . . .) Basically, Scarface and I just seemed to click in all the right ways. If it wasn't love it was an Oscar-winning performance. Even Max liked him. They played footie in the garden and Scarface took Max kite flying up on Primrose Hill. And I thought, how handy that I was in love with my upstairs neighbour. Isn't life amazing? I mean, one minute you're a sad loser thirty-recurring-year-old single mother with few friends, few prospects and a vibrator with burnt-out batteries, then wham bam and you're on an endorphin high that's out of this world and seriously considering going on contraception.

I gave him the key to my apartment.

Say no more . . .

I spotted Scarface at the bar with a spare double gin and tonic in hand and off I went, weaving in and out of tables and gathering more praise (unsolicited this time).

'So . . . what did you think of my performance?'

'Good,' he replied, kissing me full on the lips. He kissed so well.

'Only good?'

'Very good.'

'Really?' I do believe it's a girlfriend's duty to extract as many compliments as possible from her man.

'Very, very, very good.'

'Say it like you mean it.'

He blushed.

And then it clicked.

I'd had an inkling while I was on stage, although decided that he'd remained hidden in the crowd so as not to put me off.

'You missed it, didn't you?' I was outraged.

'I caught the end.' He'd promised upon pain of death he would watch me perform. 'Jerry [Scarface's boss] asked me to have a drink.'

There was a promotion in the offing. Scarface was imminently going to be declared 'senior marketing consultant' as opposed to 'marketing consultant', hence his brown nose.

'You could have brought him here.' I was so disappointed. I mean, was it too much to expect one's boyfriend to support one on the most important night of one's life?

'It's not his type of thing.'

Scarface's balls felt soft in my palms. I squeezed hard.

'I did try,' he yelped, 'honestly.'

'You bast . . .' and before I could finish my sentence, Fat Adrian bounded on to the stage to announce the winner.

Ladies and gentlemen, boys and girls, hermaphrodites, syphilitics, socialites, Shiites, Sodomites, midgets, freaks, members of the jury, council, AA, parliament, Opus Dei, IRA, the ex-Busted Fan Club and general public, it is an honour and pleasure to welcome you all to the official opening of *The Brodsky Touch*, in other words, the opposite of Midas, where everything I touch turns to shit.

You get the picture.[1]

_____

1 General warning to all readers: the following pages will be tinged in a chocolate-coloured, bitter tone (70 per cent pure lachrymose), notwithstanding a substantial amount of self-pity and a dollop of cynicism.

THE END

Every egg I ever laid went into that basket/competition.

When I heard Lisa Slater's name called out I laughed hysterically. Surely it was a joke? Who would seriously believe that Geraldine McIntosh's girlfriend and latest protégée would get into the next round of the competition instead of me? Okay, so she was a blonde, ditzy, cute, Oxbridge-educated actress-turned-comedienne with everything going for her, but my material was way better than hers and no, I wasn't just saying that.

Honestly, everyone could see it was a fix.

I demanded a recount, a retrial, a rerun. Then I feigned poor hearing and ran up on to the stage anyway. Goddamn, but that prize was mine. The audience loved my little display until they realised it was utter desperation and for real. Yes, I, the saddest clown in the world, shame-faced, walked home that night trophy-less, tail firmly tucked between my legs yet legless, having gulped back the optimistic half of a bottle of Jack Daniel's. Scarface came with me and did his best to sympathise. I forgave his non-attendance as a shoulder to cry on became a more pressing priority.

'I'm really sorry, Issy. There'll be other competitions.'

Yeah, sure, but I was a thirty-something and that something was getting on. Time wasn't on my side any more. I mean, we all have our dreams, our youthful 'look out world here I come' mind-sets. Hit thirty and those crazy dreams should have either blossomed, petered out or receded into the background of 'if only' or 'could've been' quirks of an adolescent fancy.

Let's face it, the life of a comedian tallies not with that of single motherhood, even if that mother has a steady boyfriend. The fact was that most debutante stand-ups spend three to four nights a week on the road, travelling up and down the country to gigs. Is that an appropriate life for a mother? More especially a mother who had to pay for most of the childcare.[1] Doing even one gig was costly. Do the maths: six quid an hour for babysitting plus the taxi fare home. Consider also that most comics don't start getting paid till around gig number fifty, and then it's usually only petrol money. The brutal truth was that I couldn't afford it. It was hard enough balancing work and family life, never mind performing as well.

Scarface tried to console me with, 'Things will look better in the morning.'

'Promise?'

'I promise,' he swore.

*   *   *

---

1 There was no weekend daddy on the scene, and no grandparents lurking in the wings (more like in the auditorium: Grandma was living in the States, Grandpa in Switzerland).

HOW COME MEN ARE SUCH GOOD LIARS?

In the morning I was seeing double, the hideous out-come of the previous evening magnified by two billion. Mooching about the flat like a lost soul, my spirit shattered, I was the down dog ready to be kicked, pulped, composted. Even Max, my five-year-old son, slapped his hand on to his forehead and made the L sign.

'Loser!' he chirruped.

My subsequent tsunami of self-pity freaked him out. I burst into gut-wrenching sobs, ran into my bedroom and slammed the door shut.

'Mum?' Max eased open the door to my room and stuck his lush curly head around the door-frame. 'Mum, I really don't like it when you cry,' he said.

'I know, Maxy,' I blubbered, 'but sometimes people need to let it all out [sob, sob] then things mightn't seem so [choke, choke] craaaaaaaaaaaap.'

Max skidded across the floor to my bed. Skidding was his latest craze, a by-product of scootering, though the scooter was now defunct. He'd discovered how to burn rubber by resting his foot on the brake and screeching to a halt. This practice had then been repeated to such an extent that the wheels metamor-phosed from circles to curved triangles and the scooter was rendered useless. Hence Max made do with socked feet as the fastest method of interior transport.

15

'Mum.' He was looking up at me, his cherub lips curling in distaste. 'Don't you remember anything?'

'Like what?' I asked mid-sob.

'You know?'

'Know what?'

'Chumbawamba!' he declared, like I was an idiot.

'Huh?'

' "I get knocked down but I get up again" . . . ?' He began singing the lyrics to a pop song I'd sung to him on each and every occasion he'd fallen over when he was a toddler. ' "You're never gonna keep me down." You remember?'

It had become our anthem. A mutual defiant stance at the harsh dealings life threw at Max during his first few years. At the time I called him a tumbler rather than a toddler. He was constantly tripping up, falling over or bumping into things, especially when he learned to run. On and on he would go, and keep going till he met with a wall or obstacle. The pitfalls were ever increasing, as back then he knew no fear and his padded bottom served him well. I tried my hardest not to be one of those parents forever saying 'no' to everything, or 'don't do that', otherwise known as child rearing in the absolute negative. I'd try to redirect his attention. Of course, most times I'd fail but hell, the intention was noble.

'Aw come on Mum, it's boring. "I get knocked down!" ' His small elbow nudged me in the ribs,

16

urging a response, so I dug deep and in the smallest of voices whimpered,

' "But I get up again . . ." '

BACK TO BUSINESS

Fast-forward a couple of months to Parkway, Camden, and a grotty office on the second floor of a dilapidated building. The door to the office had, as in the spirit of all great detective agencies, a frosted centre window, with the following words painted in golden italics: *The Honey Trap, Detective Agency, Marital Breakdowns A Specialty.* Directly beneath was a Ryman cardboard sign that read 'Open for Business'. If you were to cast a glance downward to the doorknob, twist it open and enter, you'd find me earnestly bitching to Nadia about Scarface.

'I don't get it.'

'I wouldn't worry, Brodsky, it's a boy thing.'

'All he had to do was call or text. It was four in the morning when he rolled in.'

Since Scarface's promotion to 'senior marketing consultant' all I ever heard was Jerry this, Jerry that, slurp, slurp, lick, lick, fawn, fawn and inevitably, 'Sorry Issy, I'm working late again tonight.' Scarface worked late more nights than not.

'Spearmint Rhino, Nads! I hate those places.'

'Don't take it so seriously, I'm sure it's just a phase.'

'Phase, schmaze. It's not on. His boss is the biggest jerk going and it makes me sick. Scarface idolises him.'

Nadia yawned loudly. I was boring her rigid; besides, she'd heard it all before. She looked at her watch: my ten-minute moaning session was running over. Time up, she signalled, and rang the miniature cow bell I'd brought back from visiting my father in Switzerland. Taking charge of the speaker's mug, a brown chipped one with the slogan 'G.K. Garages wish all their clients a very Happy Christmas 1999', Nadia announced,

'Brodsky, this is top secret and confidential.'

I was surprised. Friday afternoon 'mug time' was strictly for off-loading or moaning.

'Promise you won't tell anyone?'

I crossed my heart, swore an oath.

'Absolutely no one.'

'My word is my bond.'

'Tim and I are getting engaged.'

'What?'

Nadia, mother of two, still in her twenties (okay, so in the twilight zone), stunningly beautiful and with a voice of an angel, had met Tim a month *after* I got it together with Scarface and was now engaged to be married. How was that possible?

'Bitch!' I gasped.

'Thanks, Brodsky.'

I so had to get a handle on speaking my thoughts aloud.

'I mean, congratulations, that's marvellous news. Really . . . great.'

18

'We're hoping to get married next year. What's wrong?'

'Nothing.'

'Why are you crying?'

'An allergic reaction. It's nothing, city air pollution. I'm just so happy for you.' Sob, sob, I mean, Nads was like the younger sister I never had. Younger sisters were categorically not meant to marry first.

'Oh my God, Brodsky, remember when I had that marriage premonition . . .'

I sighed. 'And if correctly remembered, you specifically said it would be mine to Scarface.'

Don't get me wrong. I was delighted for Nadia, but I was also seething with envy. Drowning in the green stuff, my heart sank to the pit of my stomach. The state of my own relationship was hardly Elysian, never mind democratic. Actually, it wasn't really a state. We were like two territorially ambitious, neighbouring feudal warlords, between whom things were generally and fairly rotten. I stared into the mid-distance, savagely biting my nails.

'Issy, are you all right?'

'Yeah, Nads.' My lips were beginning to pucker involuntarily, then, mercifully, I was saved by the phone.

'Caller on line one, you're through to the Honey Trap. How can I help end your marriage?' I droned into the receiver.

Sure, it's a cynical business, but someone has to do it. Being an agent provocateur has taught me much

19

about the differences between men and women. There are loads, the overriding one being that men are an 'other' species and should be treated as such. From my own hypothesis (and for the record, I don't consider myself either the bitter or cynical type), it would seem, with respect to relationships 'in crisis', a man goes into his cave, but a woman goes into denial and desperately tries to amend her behaviour to suit him. A few years further down the line, post-weight loss, a whole host of new projects/hobbies, counselling, perhaps even a patch-it-up kid, the woman will eventually realise he was actually an asshole and give us a call.

Of course, it does work the other way round, though not nearly as often. We're not sexist, but in those cases (ie, men suspicious of their better halves) we just provide straightforward detecting services. The thought of being an agent provocateur in a lesbo situation was a no-go. Don't get me wrong, I wasn't lezzer-phobic. Look, we all have our own moral boundaries and girl-on-girl action lay beyond mine.

Caller On Line One was slightly taken aback by my apparent non-interest.

'Oh, I see . . . my situation is different. I'm not actually married yet.'

'Whatever, we deal with all types of relationships.'

'Good, fine, super.' She took in a deep breath and then launched into her conundrum. 'Henry, my boy-friend, actually he's my fiancé, and, well, we are getting wed soon, about to tie the knot, in the eyes of God be joined as one, this summer, a summer wedding, marquee on the lawn. I'm terribly excited, as you can imagine and . . .'

I was thinking 'cut to the chase, lady', but she didn't oblige.

Ten minutes later: '. . . since university. He studied philosophy, I read English and history, which is why we've chosen to marry in the college and, of course, he did row for Cambridge, the year they won. All the boys will be there, and you know how boys can be boys.'

Ah yes, I knew exactly where she was coming from. Flashes of Scarface spending more money on a near-naked stranger in one night than on me in the past three months raced every three seconds like a gold-fish's memory across my mind. I was rankled by his previous night's activities.

'I'd hate to think of myself as possessive or control-ling or insecure but . . .' Her voice was soft and squeaky. I imagined pale-pink lipstick and pearls. 'There is the small matter of the stag weekend coming up and . . .'

'Ahh, right.'

I'd always thought the 'last night of freedom' a strange conceit and had no understanding why it was that so many stags and hens sought to get laid on that very night. Surely any other night would be better? And in front of all your mates, too. It doesn't add up: covert behaviour should be exactly that, under cover, as it were. Call me old-fashioned, but if I ever did find myself in the position of a bride, I'd like to think it was a decision made without restraint and a state I'd want to freely enter. Otherwise, why bother?

'Don't misunderstand me, it's not that I don't trust Henry, it's just occasionally he's easily goaded into situations he wouldn't and shouldn't really be in, especially when surrounded by his peers . . .'

'I understand, Miss . . .'

'Lady Ara . . .'

'Lady Araminta Smythe-What?'

'Higson, she wants me to infiltrate the stag night and . . .'

'Undercover Brodsky as a stripper? Can't see it.' Fiona, the big boss, had flounced in, catching the tail-end of the conversation while hanging up her Burberry mac and fedora (you could so tell she had just arrived back from the Annual Great British Detectives Conference – location top secret).

Fiona was right: there was no conceivable way I could do it. I could manage burlesque at a push, but there'd have to be plenty of feathers.

'Perhaps someone else should take on the case?' she suggested. 'After all, Brodsky, you have been Honey of the Month for the past two.'

Indeed, my face – for the first time in my employment history – had adorned the monthly scoreboard. By and large it came as a result of my problems with Him Indoors, which had propelled me to focus all my frustrations on other people's husbands or partners, or just other people in general, but also I'd happened upon a case that had turned into one of the jammiest provocateur scenarios ever. It was a rich seam and one I mined copiously.

'In my opinion,' continued Fiona, 'an undercover stripper requires the body of a peachy eighteen-year-old.'

There'd been recent talk of trying out a work-experience girl. I could just envisage some über-enthusiastic school leaver with sparkling white teeth and pert breasts.

'Perhaps it's time to advertise for a younger Honey,' mused Fiona. 'We are none of us spring chicks.'

I wasn't convinced. To be a top agent provocateur one needed more than a good superficial exterior. 'In this business, Fiona, looks aren't everything,' I put forth.

'In stripping they are,' she contested.

'True . . . but . . .'

'No buts, Brodsky.'

I ceded defeat and left the office to go and check up on my . . .

JAMMY SITUATION (OR HOW I FOUND MYSELF IN ONE)

Arthur was a mid-ranking civil engineer with a nice house in Islington. His manner was obsequious, gentle in the extreme and his desire somewhat unusual. (It's always the quiet ones, hey?) Anyway, he wasn't your run-of-the-mill sexual deviant, the type who contacted the Honey Trap assuming the name of the company was a euphemism for a brothel. We were constantly hanging up on heavy breathers and, unfortunately, the occasional asthmatic. Clients such as those were strictly forbidden, but in Arthur's case I'd convinced Fiona to let me take him on.

'Fiona,' I'd levelled with her, 'the guy is a paranoiac. He just wants his fear substantiated, that's all. Nothing sordid, nothing untoward.'

Distrustful at first, she relented when he paid for 100 hours of surveillance in advance and in cash.

See, Arthur was my golden cow and how I liked to milk him. It was such easy work. I'd send him shady pictures of himself walking down the road, leaving the office, or standing awkwardly in a supermarket aisle buying tinned peas. Other times I'd plague him with nuisance calls, remaining silent on my end of the phone while he'd shout, 'I know you're out there, I know who you are,' or observe him in his daily routines, take notes, type them up and send them to him with cryptic comments. Basically, he paid me to taunt him with an ephemeral presence. As long as I remained in the shadows it was fine, and that is exactly what I did or didn't do. I soon realised that the mere threat of it worked just as well. So I'd pretend to watch. For every hour of surveillance I actually did, there were four others I claimed for. Instead of keeping tabs, I left heavy breathing on his answering machine and used the time saved to work on my comedy routine and partake in random open-mic spots across the city. Sure it was wrong, totally non-kosher and, I admit, a misuse of Maria the office babysitter (Scarface had proved completely unreliable in the babysitting department).

The last time I'd seen Arthur had been about six weeks before, at a Portuguese deli counter waiting to be served. He had a thing about herrings – loved the buggers. Anyhow, enough time had passed and been claimed for that I felt guilty and decided to check up on Mr Penn. It was clocking-off time at his office and I'd come down for a quick surveillance session before shooting off to do a five-minute gig at a nearby pub. So, as the long hand was about to hit the half-hour of five, and what with Arthur being a total creature of habit, I raised my eyes to glance at him coming out of the main doors.

Except that he didn't.

And I waited and waited.

Although I'd never pestered him on his office number before, I decided to call the reception and ask to be put through to him.

'Yes, that's it, Arthur Penn,' I repeated.

'There's no one here by that name,' the receptionist replied.

I begged her to check again.

'I'm sorry, Miss, but he definitely doesn't work here.'

*   *   *

Initially I wasn't too concerned, and over the following week revisited his offices, keeping a keen eye on the comings and goings. I suspected he might have changed jobs or gone on holiday, unless he was justifiably paranoid and everyone *was* out to get him and had indeed got him. There had to be a logical explanation, so I went to check out his house. I knocked. No response. Then I tried the neighbours. Neither was particularly helpful. Those on the right had recently moved in and as for the others, their Chinese housekeeper informed me, 'I not know. No see. Nothing. Busy. Velly busy. Goodbye, lady.'

I checked round the rear. The row of terraced houses backed on to the canal. I knew it well, having spied on Arthur from that vantage point on previous occasions. The garden looked only slightly unruly, and from this I deduced, knowing that Arthur was a committed green-fingered gardener, he couldn't have been gone too long. It was a little bit fishy, but even at that point I was still hopeful of a rational explanation.

And that was when things began to get strange. A week passed before I got round to checking the stats and records, and found out there was no Arthur Penn, or, rather, there had been an Arthur Penn, only he had died two years previously. I was used to meeting freaks in this line of business – it really does takes all sorts – but to say this new information left me feeling spooked would be an understatement.

*   *   *

26

'A GHOST . . . THERE'S NO OTHER RATIONAL ANSWER!'

'Issy, that's ridiculous,' Scarface yawned, totally uninterested in my deductions, and turned over.

'So how did he completely vanish then?'

Lying in bed, my mind was consumed by Arthur Penn's disappearance. The case seemed to be spiralling beyond my modest detecting capabilities.

'The guy I've been trailing doesn't exist any more and that's a definite certainty.'

'Talk to Fiona,' Scarface mumbled, 'or Trisha, or Nadia.'

There was no way I could tell Fiona or Trisha, considering I'd been charging for all those hours I hadn't put in.

'I told you, I can't. Aren't you listening to a word I say?'

'Issy, I'm tired. Can we talk about it tomorrow?'

'Scarface, we just spent two hours talking about your work and then the second we talk about mine, you're too tired.'

'Please don't moan at me.'

'And another thing, Scarface,' I added, 'I thought we were going to have sex tonight. We haven't had sex for ages.'

'We had sex last week.'

'Exactly, and it's Wednesday. We always have sex on a Wednesday.'

27

'I'm tired, Issy.' Scarface was really beginning to piss me off.

'Do you not fancy me any more?'

'Oh, here we go . . .' he groaned.

'What's that supposed to mean?'

'I'm tired, okay?'

'What the . . . ? Jesus, Scarface.' There I was, trying to halve my problem by sharing it with my boyfriend, while he refused to play ball. Scarface was beginning to get on my tits – or rather, at that moment I wished he *was* getting on my tits. I mean, what's the point of having a boyfriend if he wasn't going to get on . . . with me? I sighed heavily.

'Scarface, things are going to have to change between us.'

He cut me off mid-sentence and for the first time in ages we agreed.

STORMY WEATHER

The day began heavily, the air suffocating with humidity, the skies above threatening all sorts and then delivering a thunderous electric storm around lunchtime. Nadia arrived at the office drenched to the skin, to find me sucking the tip of my right thumbnail and lying in a foetal position on the office sofa.

'Brodsky.' Her voice whiplashed me back to reality.

'What? Oh, it's you. Did you get the cakes?' I moaned,

pity perceptible in my weakly pitched voice. Another week had passed, another Friday reached, another calorific overload in the offing. Nads ignored my question.

'Well?'

'I wonder what's keeping them.'

'Traffic?' I supposed.

Fiona and Trisha were on the way back from lunch with the accountant. Nadia nodded, unbuttoned her jacket and sat down, disclosing a brown-paper bag.

'Cakes!' My eyes widened. 'So, you do have them.' My hand stretched out, eager to undress the assorted pastries of their brown-paper wrapping and expose a couple of éclairs, one chocolate, one coffee, a millefeuille and low-fat blackberry muffin. I wanted the chocolate éclair; actually I wanted both éclairs. To be honest, I wanted to stuff my face with as much as I possibly could and make myself sick.

'Scarface and I broke up last night,' I mumbled.

'What's that?' Nadia threw a copy of the *Evening Standard* at me, saving the magazine section for herself, which served to aggravate me, as the magazine was the only thing worth reading, specifically the horoscopes.

'Can't I have the magazine?'

'Brodsky, this is the wedding issue,' she attested.

'Rub it in Nads, why don't you.' So she did and waved a bejewelled finger at me. I mirrored the gesture using my middle one.

'Nads, last night Scarface and I . . .'

'Issy!' she admonished, pointing at the cakes, 'Can't you wait till the others arrive?'

'They're late, they mightn't come for ages.' I had already demolished one half of the chocolate éclair and was cutting through the coffee one.

'What's the problem, Brodsky?'

'I wanted the magazine.'

'I'm reading the magazine.'

'Can't you at least read out the horoscopes?'

'Why?'

'I'm hoping to meet Mr Right this weekend.'

'You're really annoying me.'

'Nads, you're not listening.'

'Go on, then,' she snorted dryly, fast flicking through the pages.

'Scarface and I broke up.'

Silence descended; then emerged the distant whirring sound of Nadia's brain finally computing my news.

'What? What?' She looked genuinely shocked. 'When?'

'Last night.'

'Why?'

'We put it down to irreconcilable differences.'

'Irra . . . what?'

'Differences.'

'Being?'

'He's a man and I'm a woman.'

How quickly the sheen of romance fades. After glorious vistas of this thing called love comes the incessant compromising, the loss of personal space, unmet expectations, the 'where is this going?' talk, the 'you're not the father of my child' talk, the 'don't talk to my child that way' talk, the 'don't talk to me that way' talk, even the 'okay, so perhaps I am jealous of your relationship with my son' talk. Then there was the 'are you listening to me?' talk and the 'did you hear what I said?' talk, not to mention the constant petty swipes and general grief. All sprinkled with a fair bit of undermining and lastly, the 'for Christ's sake, the least you could have done was ring' talk.[1]

Sure, we'd been fighting a lot recently but, as I told Scarface, every couple has their ups and downs. Our problem was probably due to us having not enough ups and too many downs.

'Why can't you take things seriously, Issy?' he'd groaned.

'Because I'm a comedian,' I'd replied.

'That isn't funny.'

He was right. It was a naff, pathetic attempt at humour.

He said things had changed and that he didn't feel as strongly toward me as he once had.

'Jesus, Scarface,' I'd cried. 'Grow up – most people in relationships hate each other, loathe each other. We actually like each other. Believe me, that is a huge plus. The roaring fire of passion can only be sustained for so long: it changes to a flickering flame. Think of it in PlayStation terms: we are on another level.'

1 In place of the word 'talk' one could also use 'argument'.

What is it with blokes, eh? If they're not playing with one type of knob, it's another. God damn all PlayStations, God damn all knobs. God damn it all!

I never did get any on that Wednesday or, for that matter, any subsequent night.

'But what happened exactly?' Nadia flung down the magazine and rushed toward me with open arms. Oh how we girls love the nitty-gritty.

'He said he wanted some space.' Actually it was more along the lines of: 'I can't do this any more.'

'Do what?' I'd asked.

'I need a break. I think it would be better if we had a break,' he'd said.

'What do you mean?'

He'd rambled on for a bit, said he loved me but wasn't in love with me, if that made any sense. I'd wanted to smack him in the jaw with my clenched fist. He had kept asking me if I understood. It was like he wanted my permission or reassurance that he was doing the right thing.

I'd told him he wasn't just breaking up from me but also Max. He got defensive, accused me of emotionally threatening him, which I guess I was. See, I was acutely conscious of how Max might feel abandoned, and prayed Scarface would take his feelings into account. The lot of the single mum: not only do you put yourself in a vulnerable position, but your child also.

'Scarface, he's really fond of you. I don't want to see him hurt.'

'What do you suggest I do, Issy?'

'I don't know. I haven't been in this situation before.' I was sure my heart would mend, but Max really loved having Scarface around.

'He wanted out. What else can I say, Nads?'

Nadia's mouth gaped open, wherein her tongue lay retarded before she came to her senses and wailed, 'Issy, you can't let this happen. If you two guys can't make it, nobody can.' Nadia had liked Scarface. She'd said we were two of a kind and foresaw great things.

'What's Brodsky done now?' Trisha pushed open the door to the office. Trisha is like paint, either bone dry or a bit wet. She didn't suffer fools gladly, so our relationship was ever so slightly strained.

'Scarface and I have split.'

'Time to renew the Prozac prescription.'

'Trisha, this is no joking matter,' snapped Nadia, her tone quickly changing to one more consoling. 'Issy, do you want a cup of tea?'

'I'll have one,' barked Fiona, who stormed in all radiant like she'd just got lucky. 'Issy, guess who I had dinner with last night?' Her eyes twinkled mysteriously, 'Come on, guess.'

I wasn't in a frivolous mood, so meekly shrugged my shoulders.

'In a roundabout way, Ms Brodsky, I have you to thank for bringing us together again.'

'Really?' I was intrigued despite myself. Doing

good, even by default, was highly unusual behaviour for me. No point denying it: I was the office clown, butt of all jokes and general scapegoat. Perhaps I cast myself in the role. To an extent I must have. At worst the situation stank, but at best it was an inverted way of getting attention.

(The most recent things deemed my fault, which had nothing whatsoever to do with me, were:

1. Trisha losing the nail on her big toe. A nasty experience, I'll grant you. It occurred after I hung a picture on the office wall, which she claimed was crooked and then attempted to straighten. It subsequently fell on her toe.
2. Nads's car being clamped. Nadia was on a case, so I borrowed her car to drive Trisha to casualty. It was an emergency and inadvertently I'd parked in an ambulance bay, the point being I'd had to get as close to the hospital entrance as I possibly could to help Trisha hobble in. Lesson learnt: being charitable and doing good deeds cost dearly, like £100 for starters, and I was really miffed that Trisha didn't contribute something.
3. Fiona not having been laid for three months.
4. My mother's gynae problems. Yeah right, like giving birth thirty-recurring years ago could be that problematic as to continue into one's fifties?
5. Max blaming me for everything because I was his mother. True, but that's a given.)

Fiona sashayed up to my desk.

'Brodsky, last night I had dinner with Geraldine McIntosh.'

'Really?'

Fiona smiled smugly. 'Yes, really. We used to be childhood . . . sweethearts.'

'Bit odd,' I mumbled, 'considering Geraldine's a lesbo and you're . . . were a homo.'

'At the time she was a goth and I was a nerd,' explained Fiona. 'If you must know, we had a spiritual relationship, one that transcended the physical.'

'Ah, one of those,' Trisha commented. 'Where one partner is besotted and the other not interested in the slightest.'

I winced, then fleetingly wondered if Scarface could be tempted back into a relationship on such a premise.

Fiona sighed heavily. 'No, not one of those. She, eh, became an ardent man-hating feminist and we drifted apart.' Fiona gazed dreamily into the distance, then added: 'You do know she's going out with that stand-up Lisa?'

'Hmm, yes . . .' I mumbled. How could I forget?

The three of us peered across at Fiona. She was behaving as if she was sort of in love.

'So, Brodsky, I owe you one.'

And even in my anguished post-break-up state, I thought it best to take advantage of Fiona's magnanimous mood and asked if she could put in a good word for me.

'May, may not,' Fiona teased. 'Right, ladies, I'm

absolutely ravenous, where are the cakes?' Hungrily
her eyes scanned the room. Fiona hitting a sugar low
was not a happy sight. Furtively, I brushed away the
remaining crumbs from my top lip. Too late, for she
spotted the torn paper bag.

'Who's been eating the cakes?' she roared.

My arm shot up. An old habit retained from years
back, from an era when I truly believed that honesty
was the best policy.

HONESTY?

Is there such thing? How many of us are ever really
honest with ourselves, never mind others? I told Scarface he could have his break. He sought permission. I
granted his request. I reckoned I could let him run free
from the paddock awhile. He would be back, just like
Arnie. He would be. Surely fate was not so cruel as to
scathe my heart so recklessly.

And I made it my mantra, my prayer, my hail
Scarface, boyfriend of mine, bastard of the century
. . . can't we just be friends?

He said of course we could be friends, but to give it
some time.

He said he needed space, to find himself again.

He said the Kings of Leon, Raconteurs and Kaiser
Chiefs CDs were his. I had my iPod so what did I care?
Besides, he would be back. It was a guaranteed cer-

tainty, as I'd swapped the original CDs for Robbie Williams, Christina Aguilera and Westlife. Thankfully, Max's reaction to our split had been one of incredible resilience. Scarface let him keep his PlayStation and pledged Max full access to the Xbox he was going to purchase, which may have had something to do with it. Scarface also promised to continue to take Max to Sunday football until his course finished. I was really appreciative and it indicated to me that Scarface wasn't a complete bastard and hadn't disappeared into the ether.

SPEAKING OF WHICH . . .

It was Sunday morning. I'd waved Scarface and Max goodbye and decided to take the opportunity to have another look at Arthur Penn's house. This case was creeping me out big time. At present my instincts and the evidence suggested he was a spectre, a ghost, a floating soul, maybe even a Time Lord. Scarface, having scoffed at my suggestion, made matters worse by saying, 'You're making this up,' which then totally freaked me. I hadn't yet considered the notion that Arthur could be a manifestation of my own psyche.

Thus my imagination ran riot before I reined it in and gave myself a sharp slap on the wrist for even considering such nonsense. The Arthur I had followed *had* to exist, as he had paid quite a hefty sum of money for my services in advance. The payment had definitely been made. I remembered the large stuffed envelope of notes totalling a good few hundred. I checked the office account books, then rechecked, only to conclude that no record of the payment existed. I couldn't believe it! I casually mentioned it to Fiona, her response being a wink and nod. 'Cash advance? Many hundreds you say? I can't recall any cash advance. However, Brodsky, there is a fair whack now owed for all those hours you have recently claimed.'

Oh Christ, so much for our kosher book-keeping. Feeling flummoxed, I was unsure whether to call the police or a clairvoyant. If I went to the police, I'd have to prove he existed and then that he had disappeared into thin air, and vice versa with a clairvoyant. All avenues of the investigation led to blind alleys or full stops, and Arthur's mobile number and email had ceased to be. So there I was on a Sunday morning, breaking into Arthur's house in a last-ditch attempt to find some clue or remnant of his existence.

The back door opened easily. Breaking and entering was a knack I had acquired on a three-day course I'd attended (and passed with flying colours) called 'Detecting Tricks of the Trade'. Hint: it's all in the wrist action.

So in I broke.

The place was immaculate; there wasn't a speck of dust anywhere. Everything was exactly as it should be, the kitchen pristine, the hallway dust-free, the post neatly piled up on the hall table, though addressed to a Rose and James Fenton. Mr and Mrs Fenton were evident from the family pictures hanging on the walls. I walked through the rooms, scanning for some hint of Arthur's presence. There was nothing – no remnants of the bookish civil engineer with his dry skin condition, or haemorrhoid cream in the bathroom cabinet or striped shirts or the latest novel by his favourite author or . . . I was baffled, confounded, mystified and then . . . Downstairs I heard the front door open. I, in the master bedroom, momentarily froze, then dive-bombed beneath the bed. I heard faint activity from below, someone clattering about in the kitchen for perhaps fifteen minutes and then the front door slammed shut. Gripped by fear, I reckoned it was time for my getaway. Slowly, carefully, silently I crept down the stairs, easy does it. My hand on the door latch, freedom beckoned, my heart thumping against my chest with such force that I was sure I'd suffer internal bruising. The door opened . . . I was free, I was out, I was face to face with the cleaning woman from the neighbour's house, who appeared to be on her way in.

She screamed.

I screamed.

She screamed louder.

I screamed loudest and, in that high-pitched frenzy, I pushed her aside and she stumbled. 'Stop lief! Lobber, stop lobber!'

I could still hear her screaming as I fled down the steps and up the street.

THAT SPECIAL TIME OF THE MONTH

Aka the monthly office debrief meeting. No cakes this time, just strong black coffee. Attempting to explain how I, a top Honey Trapping detective, had come to lose my own client was not something I'd relish. I was rattled by recent events, kept wondering if the cleaning lady was the type to report me to the police or, worse, her own personal Triad leader, or even worse, both. As for Arthur, I had feelings of anger and abandonment mixed with powerlessness about what on earth I should do next. Tactically, I arrived late to the meeting and thankfully walked straight in on Nadia's grand announcement. Trisha and Fiona were literally frothing at the mouth, enraptured over Nadia's forthcoming wedding, all delicious in their girliness. 'What colour dress do you think you'll get? What sort of wedding are you planning? When are you starting your diet? Any honeymoon plans? What about the hen party?'

'Sorry I'm late everyone,' I apologised. 'Overslept.' My mind was so frazzled by recent events that honesty in this case was the best policy.

'The hen party . . . Ah yes, Brodsky,' sighed Fiona, 'What's happening with the Cressida case?'

40

'Cressida case?' My mind drew a blank.

'Her Ladyship?'

Araminta had been keeping me up to date with all the minute details of the forthcoming stag night. Oliver, the best man, had organised some Formula One race driving to get the action 'revving', followed by a top restaurant, all washed down with a suitably sleazy Soho cabaret. I'd checked out the joint and there wasn't much hope of infiltration. I was about ten years too old to hostess/strip, too young to madam the girls and there was no way I was going to spray people with cheap perfume in the lavvies. Attending as a lone female punter was not a viable option. 'You could do your act,' suggested Trisha.

'Pardon?'

'At the cabaret,' Trisha continued.

She was right, it was obvious. I could try to do a spot as part of the cabaret.

'You could even dress up for it.'

'How about Nanny Brodsky?' Fiona smirked.

'A schoolgirl may work better,' suggested Nads.

'No, it has to suit Brodsky's material,' Trisha elucidated. 'Your shtick . . . hmmm.' She considered the notion awhile. Funny, sexy, high energy, these were the adjectives going through my mind.

'A desperate, delusional woman,' she concluded.

Nadia laughed. 'That's it, exactly. Issy, you know I love you, but your material is so cringeworthy.' Thank the Lord I had rhino skin.

'How about a dominatrix?' Fiona was way off the radar.

'Got it!' Trisha proclaimed. 'A nurse. Do it as a nurse.'

All eyes were on me, three chins nodding in agreement.

'Nurse Issy Brodsky . . . I can see it now.'

Thing was, I could see it too. Besides which, there was no point in wasting that cheeky little nylon number I'd splashed out on in the hope of seducing Scarface into submission.

POST-SPLIT ANALYSIS

The 'break' with Scarface kept being extended. Three weeks down the line there was no hint of a reconciliation. I didn't do rejection well. Does anyone? It hung in my throat and clogged my intestines. I'd fret and have nightly horizontal workouts, twisting and turning in my bed before eventually succumbing to sleep. Scarface moved out or, rather, up. Not that he'd actually, in reality, ever moved in, though he did keep a spare pair of underpants in my knicker drawer and a toothbrush in the bathroom. In the interim I tried to pretend that we had never occurred. Haphazardly I flung my ragged emotions in the pending box 'to be dealt with later', only the hurt was a bit like facial filler and had a tendency towards seepage.

*   *   *

Peeking though the classroom window, I spied thirty five-year-olds sitting obediently with their book bags on the desks waiting for their collectors to shuffle in and claim them. Max sat at a table in the middle of the classroom. I could see him straining to catch a glimpse of me and when he did, his face beamed. Every day at 3.30pm this collector (me) was guaranteed a mile-wide smile.

'Hi Max.'

'You okay, Mum?'

'Hayfever.'

'What's that?'

'Come on, let's go.'

OR

'I can't get over losing you,' I was singing in the kitchen, preparing tea. Max was watching his favourite show of all time, *The Simpsons*, and when it was over he came to check up on me.

'Mum, why do you keep playing the same record over and over again?'

'What's that, darling?' I turned down the volume.

'Are you crying, Mum?'

'No, I was just chopping onions for dinner.'

'What are we having?'

'Fish fingers and beans.'

AND THEN

'Where are you, Mum?'

'In here.'

'Can I turn the light on?'

'Sure, come here and give us a cuddle.'

'What were you doing?'

'Just thinking.'

'Are you sad?'

'A little.'

'About Scarface?' Aghh, but aren't they just so intuitive?

'Yeah.'

'Mum, Scarface has only gone back upstairs. It's not a big deal.'

The man-to-boy talk had been very reassuring for Max. Scarface promised everything would be fine, nothing would change, and for Max, little had.

'Yeah, you're right, can I have another cuddle?'

Breaking up was such a pain. I ended up getting in touch with an old mate, one I'd dropped the minute Scarface had come on the scene (I know, but shit happens!).

'Hi God . . .

Long time no see . . .

How's it going?

It's me, Issy . . .

. . . Brodsky . . .

Sorry I haven't been in touch recently, but, well, I've been in a relationship . . .

Yeah, I know. Me in a relationship! I swear. Sure as you know yourself, anything's possible.

Look, God, I realise I'm a person of little faith and a fairweather friend and now single again, but I need your help, guidance, advice. Hello? Hello?'

Same old, same old. Men, they're never there when you need them . . . probably hanging out with his holy mates.

THE UNTOUCHABLES (GOOD NAME FOR A POLE-DANCING TROUPE, EH?)

'Ohh,' I squirmed, 'that looked sore.' The girls were just finishing up their opening act. Opening being an apt and, in their case, descriptive verb.

Reggie ran the Soho Strip Club. 'It's 110 per cent kosher,' he promised. 'Everything over board [I think he meant above board] and you,' he said, spittle flying, with his finger poking my chest, rat-a-tat-tat, 'had better be good, 'cause these guys want top entertain-

45

ment, razzmatazz, glitz.' His finger then disappeared up into his left nostril.

I had taken Trisha's advice and managed to persuade Reggie into letting me perform. The club was tiny, or rather intimate, lots of smoky mirrors and black-leather upholstery. I hadn't a clue what to expect from the cabaret line-up, but was glad to be performing fairly early on. It happened that the act before me was a woman with a smoking fanny. Believe me, that proved hard to follow. I'd heard about acts of that calibre, but had never witnessed one before and it crossed my mind that it may be a safer method of smoking. Araminta's fiancé, Henry, was in an uproarious mood. He and his gang of stags were having a wild time. The club was at their mercy, being the only group present, bar a few lone punters. Brushing down my nylon nurse's outfit, I stepped through the smoke cloud and into the spotlight.

The stags were so well brought up; they laughed in all the right places and applauded my efforts with such vigour I overran my set, enough so as to peeve off Nicola and her extraordinary Nipple-ettes, who were on next. Offstage, Reggie awarded my arse with a triumphant slap and offered me a drink. The only beverage was Champagne and, realising I had a mighty thirst on me, I accepted.

Everything was going according to plan, until I spotted Bambuss perched on a stool by the bar, his largesse spilling over the sides. Bambuss, the hirsute detective, boyfriend of the wonderful Maria (our

Honey Trap 'Bosley') was not altogether happy to see me. He was never happy to see me.

'Explain yourself,' I demanded, arms crossed.

See, the last time we had encountered one another had led to Maria and him almost splitting up when I'd accused him of being a philanderer. It occurred one afternoon when I found myself wandering in Soho prior to a coffee date with my brother and chanced upon him in Ann Summers[1] fondling lingerie, specifically a crotchless pair of panties and cupless corset. Knowing Maria would not be seen dead in such a cheap and nasty get-up, my suspicions were roused as opposed to aroused. A couple of weeks later I sighted Bambuss once more, this time strolling nonchalantly in the Soho area with his arm wrapped round a peroxide blonde.[2] Now, what would any normal law-abiding citizen think?

Exactly. So I immediately called Maria, trusty beautiful Rubensesque Maria. She was shocked, hurt, taken aback, stunned as I relayed to her the grimy details. Hand on my heart, I swore to the Lord above that I'd witnessed her Bambuss, the love of her life, her paramour and more, cavorting with a dirty street prostitute during daylight hours. Holding back on none of the seedy details, I gave it to Maria straight.

1 Listen, I was only in there as my Bunny had come with a lifetime guarantee.
2 As above. What lifetime, I wondered, were they measuring in? A flea's? I demanded my money back.

Okay, so I did embellish the story a wee bit, but it was negligible, mere word aesthetics.

'Perverted sex stuff. I swear to you Maria, I wouldn't say this unless I thought it best you knew about it.'

'What stuff?'

'Crotchless panties, pornish in style, baby-doll nighties, titty tassels. As if you'd wear that in a million years.'

Turned out I was wrong.

'Issy, you big prude,' she giggled.

'No way!' I gasped. 'I didn't think they did that stuff in your size.'

'What you mean "my size"?'

Damn me and my big mouth. 'Nothing. I meant . . . nothing, Maria, but what about the prostitutes I saw him with?'

'What string of floozies?' Bambuss yelled at me in defence of his reputation and relationship. 'On my mother's mother's mother's moustache I swear, I haven't looked at another woman since meeting Maria.'

'Really, Detective? Then answer this, what precisely were you doing on Wednesday, 7th April, between the hours of noon and half past in Brewer St with your arm linked to a woman of ill repute?'

Turned out he was arresting her.

'Look, we all make mistakes,' I appealed to their senses of both mercy and forgiveness, even contested that the undue suspicion I'd planted on their relationship could easily be redirected and shaped into a heavy douse of passion, or a trust test, thus cementing their love for one another. They didn't buy it.

Now Reggie was standing at my side pouring a flute of Champagne. Here was my opportunity to prove to Maria that Bambuss really was a low-down dirty dog.

'So, Detective Bambuss, what excuse are you going to use this time?'

'Brodsky, my dear,' he snarled at me between clenched teeth, 'I'm on a job, get lost.'

'Yeah right. I may look like one, but I'm not a complete idiot, Detective.'

Meanwhile Reggie, having heard me utter the word 'detective' twice, had become quite excited.

'Out, fatso, out of here now before I call the . . .'

POLICE RAID

Araminta was sobbing down the phone.

'You've ruined my life, Issy Brodsky.'

'Look, Lady . . . erm.'

'Araminta.'

'Look, Lady Araminta, you asked me to do a job and that's exactly what I did. Okay?'

'I'm afraid it's not okay. Henry's reputation has been sullied. His whole future in politics could be affected.'

This dame was driving me nuts.

Bambuss turned out to be telling the truth, again. He and the boys in blue had uncovered a ring of Albanian women in a 'massage parlour' run by a man known as Vlad. A tip-off led them to Reggie's club and they had been casing the joint for weeks. Apparently it was a place Vlad felt comfortable trading flesh in. On the night in question, after I'd blown Bambuss's cover, a kerfuffle ensued, followed by an outright brawl. The stags had thought it was all part of the evening's entertainment, an updated version of a Western cowboy saloon scene, which only served to make matters worse, and the evening ended with the club being wrecked and everyone hauled down to the station.

'It's shameful. Mumsy has had to take to her bed. It's prompted one of her migraines. She is of a nervous disposition, you know.'

Dear oh dear, I thought, how tragic. I could hear Lady A sniffing.

'Don't you think you are being a tad over-sensitive. After all, they weren't arrested, merely cautioned.'

Lady A wasn't the only one pissed off. The performers were livid. Raids were only acceptable at the end of an evening. They held me personally responsible for their loss of earnings, ditto Reggie, and they were threatening action.

'What type of action, Reggie?' I asked. 'Live?'

'Oi,' he sneered, 'what are you? Some sort of joker?'

*   *   *

50

PROCRASTINATION

The office windows were wide open, time once again for rising dust and the stressful sound of homebound traffic. Maria was picking Max up from school, allowing me do a full day's work. An unhindered day without the school pick-up – glorious. I managed to get more things done during that time than at any other day in the week. Of course, with each passing year it had become in many ways so much easier to look after Max but, and there was always a but, now my chauffeuring abilities were constantly under strain, as I had to ferry Max hither and thither to his extracurricular activities, play dates and parties.

It was touching six. Trisha sat opposite me giving herself a French manicure and Fiona was on the internet looking for a present for Nadia's forthcoming engagement party.

'We could get her some silk sheets,' Fiona suggested, obviously bored with her task.

'I already told you,' I sighed, 'she wants cash.'

'I hate giving cash, it's too impersonal and Nadia is our number-one Honey,' stated Trisha.

'Excuse me?' and I pointed to the picture on the Honey of the Month award board. 'What about me?'

'Brodsky, a) that's not you and b) that was ages back.'

Jeez, but Trisha was right. I mean, where does the time go? One minute it's mid-March and the next it's the end of June. High summer was upon us.

'Brodsky, I've been meaning to ask what happened with the Arthur Penn case.'

'Er, what?' Damn, but there a huge lump under the carpet by my feet. Detective Tip Number 514: When in doubt, do nowt. I'd let things simmer awhile, out of sight, out of mind. Procrastination was my order of the day.

'Oh, it's going fine,' I lied.

'Really? 'Cause according to your worksheets, he now owes us close on 300 quid.'

'What?' I near choked on the thought. This was all I needed. I couldn't believe I'd misused or, rather, misappropriated that many hours of office time.

'When was the last time you saw him?'

'Thursday just gone.' I gabbled, fist in my mouth. I forgot someone had to pay for all those hours. I knew it was wrong, tantamount to thievery of time. 'Tea, anyone?' I nervously offered.

Fiona eyeballed me suspiciously. 'Tea?' she gasped. 'Brodsky, it's after six, time to go.'

Home time, the weekend was upon us. Post-Scarface, I dreaded the weekends. They had a tendency to be long and lonely. In the office kitchen I stalled, rinsing the week's supply of mugs that gathered on my desk obscuring my workload, and fretted over Arthur's case. I wondered if I should come clean, or delay awhile and then in a couple of weeks say he'd absconded, or if I should borrow money from the Honey Trap and promptly return it as payment . . . Such were my scattergun thoughts, when amidst this I caught snippets of a conversation.

'Blind to it. Smitten,' Fiona was explaining to Trisha.

'I understand. When Tony had the au pair . . .'

'A total bitch . . . Had me thinking, she's going in to hospital . . . so maybe the girlfriend . . .'

'Anything's possible.'

'You're right, but it puts me in an awkward position. I don't want to be held accountable.'

'Set her up.'

Fiona had been pacing the small office floor and then, hearing the water flow down the waste, popped her head around the screen partition separating the workplace from the cubbyhole kitchen.

'Brodsky, you still here?'

'I was just washing up,' I stuttered, my voice faltering.

'Oh right. We thought you'd gone ages ago.'

Indeedy, and I got the distinct impression from her blushing cheeks that perhaps I shouldn't have overheard that conversation. There was a long, uncomfortable pause.

'Guess I'll go then . . .'

THEN . . .

A couple of days later Fiona was screeching down the phone at me.

'Brodsky, I've done you a favour. I got you a gig.'

'You what?'

'A gig, you heard.'

'Oh brilliant. Wow, right, well that's great!' I enthused, hardly believing my luck. Fiona had come up trumps. I'd been doing my utmost to keep my hand in with the comedy. Any chance to perform and I jumped.

'And Brodsky, this is not just any gig.' At the very last moment someone had pulled out of the finals of the 'Women Can Be Funny Too' competition. I couldn't believe it and had Max pinch me in case I was dreaming.

'Ow . . . okay, stop it, Max,' I yelped. 'So, when is it?' It was literally a last-minute thing. Fiona was calling me from the pub.

'You've got fifteen minutes to get yourself into that nurse's outfit and down here.' Geraldine needed an opening act and pronto.

'But . . . but it's a school night, what about Max?'

'Can't you palm him off on somebody?'

'No, there's no one at such short notice.'

'Brodsky, fame costs, get yourself a bloody baby-sitter for Chrissakes.'

'I can try ringing a few people, but it will take time to organise.'

'Bring him along. I'll buy him a Coke, that should keep him quiet.' (Ha, I thought, one sip of Coke and Max went into hyperdrive. Fiona might have acquired the outward apparatus of a woman, but at the core she was still a man, and one with zero maternal instincts.) I gathered up Max and rushed to the pub.

FIFTEEN MINUTES LATER

Max was hyperdriving Fiona mad. I left them in the downstairs bar, where she was doing her best to keep him from playing Human Tornado, where the aim of the game was to destroy whole rooms in seconds by ricocheting off the walls.

'Maxers, I'll be upstairs for ten minutes tops,' I promised. 'You stay here with Fiona, okay?'

He growled and gave me the evil eye. He didn't like Fiona and wasn't afraid to show it. 'Fiona, Mum said you used to be a man, can you play football?'

'No, Max, I can't play football, now drink your Coke.'

I ran up the stairs. Fat Adrian, the MC from the previous competition gig, was already on stage warming up the audience. Geraldine stood by the door and, as I entered, took me aside and said, 'I appreciate this, Issy, thanks very much.'

'Not a problem, it's a great opportunity for me.' I went for the schmoozy stance and commentated, 'Unusual for someone to let you down at the finals.'

'It was Brillo Boy,' she explained. 'Called away to a last-minute audition. Fiona mentioned you were on your way down, suggested I give you another chance.' She winked at me. 'It was a very close call last time, Issy.'

'Thanks Geraldine. I'll try not to let you down.'

'Brilliant!' bawled Minger One.

'Fabulous,' added Minger Two. The Mingers were a Liverpudlian sister act, strong in accent and repartee. I knew them vaguely from the circuit. They were outrageous and definitely bound for Edinburgh. Both gave me a joyous double thumbs-up. 'Good on you, girl,' they cheered as I ran off stage. 'Nice one.'

'Thanks,' I feigned modestly. The gig had gone well, miles better than anticipated, probably due to less fretting time.

'You hanging around?'

'Can't, my five-year-old is downstairs.'

'Bummer, we're going to get blasted, have an ace night of it. Go on, stay for a few,' they implored.

'No really, I can't.'

Sure, it would have been nice to stay for a few drinks, relax, let my hair down but, fact was, being a mum, I couldn't. Motherhood had a way of interfering with my social life. Thus, as quickly as I'd arrived, I left, this time without waiting to hear Adrian announce the winner.

*   *   *

'Shut up, Max!' I screamed. 'I can't hear myself think!' Max had been playing Green Day's 'American Idiot' non-stop for the past hour.

'Sorry, Fiona, what did you say?' I shouted into the receiver.

'I'd like to have a one-to-one with you, Issy.'

The dreaded one-to-one. I lived in fear of the one-to-one. In my experience it was never a good thing and usually ended in me being let go, or made redundant or promoted to retirement. It spelt out Jobseekers' Allowance.

'Damn Fiona, I'm really busy, my diary is completely full for the next few weeks. What about . . .'

A time and a place were agreed.

Mine, an hour later.

MINE, AN HOUR LATER

I suspected that she suspected something was amiss vis-à-vis the Arthur Penn case. I could think of no other outstanding discrepancies. It was Nadia's engagement party later that evening and I was in the kitchen ironing my least shabby of dresses and a pair of Max's combats. I didn't hear the doorbell go. Max let Fiona in and the next thing I knew, she was peering over my smalls. She struck an imposing figure dressed head-to-toe in Jaeger, which suited her long, shapely legs and fine, broad shoulders. I reprimanded Max for opening the door to potential strangers.

'But I recognised his voice,' Max shouted back provocatively. He really did not like Fiona and then, to further agitate, waved his Game Boy at me, knowing full well he had already used up his daily time-quota.

'Domesticity suits you,' Fiona smiled and then asked if I could whip up a little something for her, as she was absolutely famished. I offered her chicken nuggets, which she accepted.

'So, to what do I owe this honour, Fiona? Let me guess: you've discovered some major discrepancy on my part?' I asked in a mock-amusing tone (Rule Number 568, Article B, Subsection III of *Detecting: A Way of Life*: In certain situations pre-emption can be a lifesaver).

'Why, should I have?'

'Eh, well no, but . . .'

'Agh, yes, Brodsky, I've been meaning to ask you about the Arthur Pe . . .'

'Who?' (Rule Number 569, Article B, Subsection IV of *Detecting: A Way of Life*: Always feign ignorance when under attack.)

'The Arthur Penn case,' she pronounced with crystal-clear diction.

'All under control,' I blurted.

'I think I saw him the other day.'

'Really?' I gasped, far too interestedly not to invoke suspicion. 'You actually saw Arthur?'

'Pretty sure, at least he looked identical to the man in the pictures you took.' Of course, the pictures . . . I still had the negatives.

'It was him, he was in the Portuguese deli round the corner, but Brodsky, we need that bill settled.'

'Eh, right. Arthur loves his herrings.'

I was half-tempted to come clean and tell Fiona about the case, but the reality was I'd definitely be sacked if the truth came out. And then the microwave bell pinged and I laid down before Fiona a plate of chicken nuggets and baked beans and Fiona laid down before me a proposition so phenomenally life-changing that I then lay down at her feet and kissed them, coinciding with Max appearing at top skid-speed.

'Yeughhh, Mum,' Max blasted, 'you are so gross.'

THE ENGAGEMENT PARTY

In combative mode, Max was playing Human Tornado again, having been given a Coke by one of Nadia's kindly relatives. The happy couple had rented a room above a pub and filled it with family, friends and assorted M&S canapés. Feeling peckish, I had appropriated a corner of the table. Nadia and Tim were glowing, the entire place high on their transparent joy. It made me wonder if I should have tried harder with Scarface. My brows furrowed, pondering on the things that really matter, like family, friends, relationships. It was unsettling to be single again. I was back in that social limbo, unable to fit in with 'couples' or baggage-less singletons. The former perceived me as a threat, or the unknown quantity. Neither did I fit in with the latter group as, due to the confines of motherhood, I couldn't go out at the drop of a hat or stay out all night as others did.

'You okay, Issy?'

'Huh?'

'You look a little distracted.' Trisha had arrived with her boyfriend Pete, a younger man she'd met at the gym. Trisha, a divorced mother of three, was the quintessential workout-aholic, with an amazing body for a forty-four-year-old. Post-Scarface, she had offered to get me a discounted membership at her gym, as my endorphins plummeted and I broke out in zits.

'Really, Issy, you should go the gym, you'd feel so much better,' she advised.

'Never seem to find the time,' I responded.

'It's the perfect place to meet someone,' she whispered. 'You're not going to meet anyone here.'

It was depressing to be surrounded by a room full of couples. The behaviour was fairly predictable; for one thing, the sexes usually segregated halfway through events, the women ended up talking to the women, men to the men and there's scarce a chance of any type of flirtation. At the time though, it wasn't men that were on my mind. It was Fiona's proposition. I couldn't think of anything else. So portentous was her proposal, I was in a state of shock.

'Cheer up, Brodsky, you'll find someone.'

'Yeah, yeah, whatever.'

Nadia merrily drifted over. 'Issy, there's been something I've been meaning to ask you,' she said. 'I have a huge request . . . a really big favour.'

Oh my God, just like buses. Never sight nor sound of one, then along come two in a row. Immediately my eyes narrowed, sceptical of Nadia. Her favours had the knack of becoming incredibly time-consuming, -wasting or complicated.

'The answer is no.'

'Issy, you don't know what I'm going to ask yet.'

Since the wedding announcement I sensed our friendship had been changing, and not for the better. It seemed there was distance growing between us. It felt like I was losing her to Tim: she'd jumped shelf from singleton to commitment, a state I scorned due to my recent Scarface experience.

Nadia cleared her throat.

'Issy Brodsky, my best friend ever, I would be honoured if you would be my chief bridesmaid.' In one swoop she put all my negative thoughts to shame.

'What?'

'Chief bridesmaid.'

I was astonished. 'Nadia, you have no idea how much that means to me. I never thought I'd ever be a bridesmaid.' Tears sprang to my eyes and I threw my arms around her and whisked her about the dance floor.

'Look, it's quite a responsibility, there's lots to do. We'll have to start planning stuff immediately.'

'Why? You're not getting married till next year.'

'We brought the date forward. We're going for a September wedding.'

'In a couple of months. But . . . ?'

My heart sank, unsure I could accept Fiona's proposition and be a bridesmaid for Nadia.

'There is a reason,' Nadia was prattling on. 'Promise not to tell anyone, especially Fiona and Trisha?'

'Promise.'

'I'm serious, Brodsky, I don't want to jeopardise my job.'

'What, what? Damn it, why did you bring the date forward?' The more I thought about it, the less possible it seemed that I could undertake both roles. 'You haven't got a record contract or something?' I asked her. Although her band Silver Rider had split up, Nadia was beginning to work as a session vocalist and it was only a matter of time before she found some trendy producer to whisk her off to superstardom.

'No, Issy, I'm pregnant.'

'Oh no!' I blurted out.

'Thanks.' Nadia stood back, blatantly hurt by my reaction.

'Nads,' I bit my lip, 'I mean, congratulations, but if you're getting married in a couple of months, then I don't think I'll be able to be your chief bridesmaid.'

It's always the way, eh? You plan something and then some other temptation appears in your path and you realise you can't be in two places at the same time.

You also have no excuse, 'cause your tongue gets tangled, your cheeks redden and you draw attention to yourself, and in the mid-distance you spot your two bosses raising their glasses, when the bride to be, who is on an emotional overload anyway, due to being pregnant and what have you, starts to blubber . . .

'Brodsky, you're such a bitch.'

See what I mean about the touch? Well, how about this – the day actually got worse. I left the party soon after, using the extraction excuse that Max had to be in bed by six-thirty. Nadia was upset, yet I couldn't explain myself, as I'd promised Fiona that until all the boxes had been ticked, etc, I wouldn't. Obviously, I was gagging to tell someone and my first thought was Scarface. He was the perfect person to whom I could reveal my momentous news.

There hadn't been a peep out of him for weeks. He'd gone to ground and not one glimpse of him caught. Glad, yet pissed off about it, I'd wanted to see him but pretended to myself I didn't. He plagued my thoughts twenty-four/seven. In essence he was like a virus. He made me feel sick.

Having knocked on his door, called and texted twice (okay, three or four times), I decided to wait for him on the stairs. It was a lovely summer evening. Around 1.30am Scarface arrived home.

'What you doing, Brodsky?'

'Nothing.'

'Are you locked out?'

I was sitting on the steps with a glass of wine in my hand.

'Just pretending I live in a brownstone in Manhattan.'

'These stairs are inside,' he pointed out.

Okay, so not so cool.

'Scarface, I wanted to . . . mmm . . . Well, I was wondering if . . .'

'Issy, don't do this . . .'

'I need to talk to you. I have some amazing news.'

I was blocking his passage up the stairs.

'Please can I get by now, Issy?'

'Password is?'

'Issy, I'm not in the mood.'

You know when you do something so very embarrassing you are going to be cursed by its memory for the rest of your life.

'Go on, just guess the password,' I teased, forcefully flirty.

'No.'

I refused to budge. His options dwindled and, in a manner most derisory, he said, 'Okay, I bet it's something like: "I'm sorry Issy, I was wrong," or, "Issy is always right," or, "I am a twat."'

'It was, "I love you."'

'It's over, Issy.' He heaved a sigh. 'Now let me pass.'

And I thought, 'Bastard, what a total bastard.'

*   *   *

As instructed by Fiona, I went to meet Geraldine the following day at a Pizza Pronto. Fiona's 'proposal' concerned Geraldine McIntosh and Lisa. Yes, the very same Lisa who stole the competition from me, who wrenched the title from out of my grasp. Edinburgh was looming and, for the first time in twenty years, Geraldine was unable to attend, due to an operation she was booked in to have.

'Brodsky, I've never felt this way about anyone. Anyone,' Fiona had reiterated, stuffing her face with chicken nuggets, the passion in her voice apparent. 'Let's just say Lisa has to go and this is where you come in.'

Fiona suggested that the most effective, efficient way to ascertain whether Lisa was cheating on Geraldine was to have someone on the inside follow her. To chaperone her as it were. In the form of direct inter-ventionist detection, the ideal scenario would be a comedienne doubling up as a private detective. Get the picture? 'Someone to keep an eye on Lisa in Edinburgh: not so much keep an eye on, but an eye out for. Do you understand what I'm getting at, Brodsky?'

I nodded, 'As long as you don't want me to give her the eye.'

'What are you saying?'

'Look there'll be no lesbo agent provocateur action.'

Fiona laughed. 'I doubt you're her type.'

'You know what I mean.'

'Brodsky, I want you to set her up. She's taking Geraldine for a ride, using her. I want evidence. I want Geraldine to know.'

'Why?'

'None of your business.'

'I get you, discretion is key.' Reassuringly, I tapped the side of my nose.

'Whatever it takes to get the evidence, just do it. And in return, Brodsky, you get your wish come true, to perform up in Edinburgh.'

I didn't exactly know how Fiona had managed to get me a place in the show, but the fact was she had. My big transgender of a fairy godmother boss had sat in my kitchen picking bits of chicken nuggets from out of her teeth while I jumped for joy and strummed my air guitar.

'Fiona, you have no idea how much this means to me.'

'Brodsky, for God's sake sit still. Your job is to keep schtum, got it? Lisa mustn't suspect a thing. Geraldine is not to suspect a thing. No one is to suspect a thing.' Fiona was indeed one of the most duplicitous people I had ever come across, thus an extraordinary undercover detective.

'A pretty good idea, don't you think, Brodsky?'

Of course it was a good idea. It was the most brilliant, most amazing, incredible mutually beneficial idea. Label me a mercenary, condemn me as an opportunist, but Geraldine McIntosh's cloud was to be my silver lining.

'You are so devious, Fiona,' I had smirked.

'I know,' she'd replied. 'Thanks.'

Geraldine was running late. I sat in Pizza Pronto anxiously chewing my nails, my face contorting due to the magnitude of pressure bearing down on me. My thoughts were focused on Edinburgh, on my future, and Fiona's somewhat morally reprehensible offer. Fiona had said to think of it as a proper 'inside job' and of her as my 'client'. I was merely doing a job, the payoff being a place in the show. The young waiter hovering before me coughed, then handed me a menu. He was gorgeous and I was leering. Yes, the pendulum had swung so far that I was now the guy who stares like a prat at the pretty waiting staff, much to the irritation of his partner (that's feminism for you!). Worse still, I'd become the type of twerp who then tried to make a witty comment, by way of a flirt.

'Can I get you anything, Miss?' he asked sweetly.

'What I want is off-menu,' I giggled.

He blushed profusely and was saved by Geraldine's entrance.

'Issy, there you are. Sorry I'm late.'

She swooped in, out of breath, demanding, 'A litre of sparkling, darling boy,' and lit a cigarette. The heavy smoking, late nights and rock-and-roll lifestyle had definitely taken their physical toll, though she was still a strong-looking woman.

'Ah, the lure of youth,' sighed Geraldine, indicating

the waiter who had since scarpered. 'And I should know . . .'

When Geraldine McIntosh fell for Lisa Slater, she fell hard. I understood. The magnetic lure of a flawless complexion, a bright pair of eyes that instinctively pulls on you, leaving you intoxicated beyond redemption. The blank page of youthful beauty aching to be written on, scrawled over, blotted. Even Max recognised this universal aesthetic. He had already been smitten by several babysitters and waitresses. The first time I accused him of liking his nursery teacher, he punched me, accompanied by a 'Mummm . . . shut up' denial, angry at having been caught out. I dare say I deserved it. Luckily for him, it was mutual and she was infatuated with his bowl-cut blond hair, piercing blue eyes and utter gorgeousness.

As regards Lisa, Geraldine had reached the point of saturation or in culinary terms, she was deep-fat-frying in love. Over a couple of pizzas and a decent bottle of Chianti, Geraldine talked ceaselessly about her muse and her devotion to this young, vibrant, talented, vulnerable, wild woman.

'Yes, but is she funny?' I blurted out, then added for good measure, 'It's just I find a sense of humour vital in relationships.'

'She is everything to me,' she replied, slightly stunned by my query.

All I heard was Lisa, Lisa, Lisa and then I heard, 'Right, down to business, so are you up for it, Issy Brodsky? The Edinburgh Festival?'

'Yes, most definitely, certainly, I am so excited!' I declared.

'Wonderful stuff. It's great to have you on board.' She leaned across the table and gently touched my forearm. 'And Issy, I know you'll get on fine with Lisa.'

'Don't worry, I'll keep a good eye on her,' I winked.

'What d'you mean?'

'Eh . . . nothing untoward, just being big-sisterly.'

'Oh yes, you are quite a bit older than her.'

And then we got down to the nitty-gritty.

'There's Adrian, the Mingers, Lisa and now you. We'll be doing a couple of preview shows before Edinburgh, but that's about it. Any questions?'

I sat dumbly trying to take it in. Act cool, Brodsky, like it's no big deal, as if things like this happen all the time.

'No questions,' I replied confidently, though my voice was quite highly pitched. Then Geraldine unveiled the contract and laid it out on the table. Reader, I looked down at MY FUTURE, then hollered at the waiter for a pen and, having an aversion to all legal documents, skimmed over the details and scrawled my signature at the bottom. Yes, yes, indubitably, irrevocably, most certainly, undoubtedly, yes.

I, Issy Brodsky, of sound mind and limited experience as a stand-up comic, agreed to perform a nightly ten-minute gig in the comedy show 'The Late Night Titter Club' produced by Geraldine McIntosh at the Edinburgh Fringe Festival and agreed also to undertake the following duties: leafleting, organising, liaising, and any other as yet unspecified jobs. Suitable accommodation would be provided.

Basically, that's how it happened. How the dream suddenly sprouted into another dimension, that of reality.

I ran all the way home, felt like I was in some 1950s Technicolor musical. I wanted to spin round lampposts, leap on cars, burst into song, join arm-in-arm with the common people, take over the traffic and high-leg it up Camden High Street, can-can style.

As Bob the builder said: 'Can you do it?'

'Yes I can.'

Or rather, hypothetically speaking I could, but practically – well, that was a whole other story.

A WHOLE OTHER STORY

Once upon a time in the land of domestic bliss there lived a woman who had obligations (Max), responsibilities (Max), certain duties (mothering) and a dream. She had worked long and hard for her dream. It had taken a while to surface, years of being directionless (university, post-grad, France/heartache, working as a researcher/assistant in various production companies) followed by a pregnancy, single motherhood, and in truth she knew not where the years had gone except that time marked her face and Botox was becoming a more attractive option. Then the unexpected happened and an opportunity fell, plonk, into her lap. One so portentous that she felt as if a million doors had swung open, wherein she espied her glorious future, her dream come true. But there was something niggling at the back of her mind and that something was known as her Conscience.

The major flaw in her grand plan.

Ecstatic with renewed hope she triumphantly declared, 'Nothing is impossible.'

Her Conscience snidely let pass, 'Dream on, lady. What about your obligations?'

'What about him?' she countered.

'He needs looking after.'

'He will be looked after.'

'By whom?'

'Where there's a will,' she replied, 'I'll find a way.'

'You're on your own. Really, who is going to take on the Responsibility?' If there was one thing in her life she was confident about, that was raising her Responsibility. Responsibility was a most well-rounded, confident, happy, bright funny, luscious, small person. Sure, it still astonished her that he had chosen to come through her.

'I told you, I'll find a way.'

It wasn't that she'd overlooked the fact that someone would have to take over her duties. It was just she thought she would have been given more planning time. God damn, but if ever there was a reason to live in a more conventional set-up and have a partner, then that was it: access to on-tap childcare cover.

Aha, she thought, not to be undone at such an early stage, and stated to her Conscience she would carry her Responsibility with her. After all, Responsibility was hers and would be on summer holidays.

'As a burden,' scoffed her Conscience. A month's sojourn in Edinburgh was not a place for a young child who needed constant amusement and looking after. Responsibility was not a thing to be shunted willy-nilly, here and there without due care or consideration. What kind of time was he going to have? Her Conscience continued to mock her.

'The organisation would be huge. Perhaps for a week, but not four.'

'You are forgetting that my mother is coming for the whole of August to visit.'

A chink of blue in the overcast sky where storm clouds quickly gathered.

'I doubt being a twenty-four-hour babysitter is part of her plan.'

'No, but . . .' There had to be a way around it. She considered hiring an au pair, a childminder.

'Exorbitantly costly. You should know, especially seeing as you have all that money to repay.' Her Conscience carped on as if purposefully putting obstacles in her path. Her eyes narrowed in determination. She would overcome this impediment.

'Get out of my head,' she hollered.

'Don't be pathetic. I'm your Conscience.'

'But I'm doing nothing wrong, I'm following my dreams,' she urged defensively.

'You're a mother. Sometimes I think you're living in a fantasy world.'

Outwardly she balked, though she knew it had a point. She would give her Conscience that much. Her Conscience was conspiring against her. It was undermining her.

'Tut, tut, tut, such a bad mother, thinks she can get away with having a life of her own. Tut, tut, tut.'

Suddenly she was gripped by the fear that she would lose this opportunity. 'Noooooooooo . . .' she cried out. 'Noooooooooo . . .'

'Are you okay Mum?' Max was beside me in the bed. I sat bolt upright and switched the bedside lamp on.

'Max, I was having a nightmare.'

'Don't worry Mum, there's no such thing as monsters.'

Ah, how quickly the tables turn.

THE POSITIVE SIDE OF NOT BEING AN ORPHAN

. . . is not only having a mother and a father, but parents who take an active, if at times interfering, role in Max's life. My mother lived in New Mexico and visited us for a month each year. Coincidentally, that

73

month was August and my father, based in Switzer-land, in recovery from his second divorce, was always visiting, be it on business trips and/or just for a change.

When I lost the 'Women Can Be Funny Too' quarter-final, my mother spent two hours on the phone trying to 'heal' me. My mother was an old-time hippie. A right-on, liberal, look-on-the-bright-side-of-everything do-gooder, believing in freedom of expression, peace, yoga, pictures of rainbows, positive affirmations and all things holistic, mystic and organic. Her philosophy was to be yourself, be who you wanted to be, or both. She believed in facing the fear, feeling the fear and fighting the fear – and if that didn't work, running away. Defiantly she avowed, 'What will be, will be,' yet was also convinced you could achieve anything if you put your mind to it. Dedicated to helping victims of society, she had adopted three old people in Africa (a leper, a blind woman and a cripple), two families in India, a sperm whale, an endangered species and a thousand-year-old tree.

To me this spelt out a certain neediness in her. Once I'd told her, 'Ma, you can't buy love,' to which she replied, 'Issy, where did I go wrong?'

DON'T GET ME STARTED

See, growing up wasn't all tepees and roll-ups. My folks divorced when my brother and I were little. My father went off to rake in big bucks and hide from the tax man in Switzerland, while my mother raked over her organic plot and hid her cannabis plants from the law. You could say our upbringing was privileged yet unconventional. I loved my mother dearly, but put us under the same roof for more then a couple of days and we'd be at one another like itching powder. She was too much into the alternative. No one wants their mum collecting them from school wearing rings on her fingers and bells on her toes. I was convinced that enforced vegetarianism was tantamount to child abuse, and allowing Freddie, my brother, to wear make-up so as he could express his feminine side was pathetic, considering that when I did it, I was somehow subscribing to a misogynistic, patriarchal way of life. Plus, making me wear dungarees to my non-uniform school when I was in primary was fine, but fundamentally cruel in secondary. Then, in my fourth year of secondary school, she totally went overboard and refused to let me go to Robert Henson's party, when (wait for it) I knew for a fact he actually fancied me and that I was guaranteed a snog.

As far as I was concerned she owed me one, so I called my mother and said, 'Mamushka, to whom I owe my very life, I want thou to know I will care for you unconditionally in years to come, when your bones weaken and thou descends to frailty in both body and mind. Or if beset by sickness, I give you my word that I shall tend to you as you did me in the early years, mop your brow, do the zimmer shuffle or at the very least put you in a nice enough rest home.'

'Darling, I'm touched, but what is it? You said it was an emergency.'

I cut to the chase. 'You know how I lost that comedy competition to go to Edinburgh?'

'Yeah . . .'

'Well, it just so happens the promoter has offered me a ten-minute slot in her show and . . .'

'Issy, I thought this was an emergency. I'm in the middle of a three-day detox deep meditation. I'll call you back.'

I called my father. He said, 'Marvellous news, darling,' and he'd think about it.

I decided to think more laterally.

I called my brother.

He refused to take my call.

I called Fiona.

'There could be a problem with the childcare cover,' I said.

'Find a solution,' was her riposte.

Trisha said, 'Do you want me to take over the Arthur Penn case, 'cause we are not a charity.'

Maria said, 'I'd love to but . . .' There's always a but, and hers was a summer cruise.

Nadia said, 'Apology accepted,' having scoffed the entire box of Rococo Chocolates I'd bought for her and then said, 'Issy, about being chief bridesmaid for us.'

'Nads, I already told you, I don't think I have the time.'

'And we respect your decision. See Tim and I were thinking that maybe you're too old.'

'Old?'

'You are thirty-something . . .'

'Nads, what has age got to do with it?'

'It's going to look weird with you and Kassie.'

'What d'you mean?'

'She's eight and you're . . .'

'Not.'

'We just think it's going to look strange.'

'Oh do "we". Chrissakes, Nads, can't you see what's happening to you? You're beginning to speak in the plural.'

'I'm getting married!'

'Fine, it's your wedding, do what you want.'

'I will, thanks.'

However, more daunting than not having any confirmed child cover was our first preview show. Crossing the bridge at Little Venice to the famous Canal Café Theatre, it struck me that I was the show's last-minute appendage and Festival virgin, and as such I'd probably be expected to partake in some form of an initiation ritual. Geraldine had suggested we turn up early so we could rehearse. I was first to arrive and sat in the small, dark theatre awaiting the others. Soon Adrian bounded up the stairs, his huge presence swallowing up the space. Adrian Down was a big man. A big, wide man, a bit like Hagrid's little brother.

'Hi Issy, you're very early.'

'Enthusiastic,' I replied. 'Plus I need the practice.'

'Well congratulations, babe. I knew you'd make it.'

'Thanks, though it was a close call.' Inwardly I felt like such a cheat, my place in the show begotten by ill gains.

'The nurse's uniform is great. Now it's just your material you have to work on.'

'Ha ha, Adrian, I am only a novice . . .'

If I was a comedy cocker spaniel pup, springy tail wagging and recently house-trained with a nose still wet with my own urine, then Adrian was a big German shepherd of a dog. He'd been in the business as an MC and stand-up long enough to know everyone from the newcomers to the old-timers to the in-betweeners, the continual try-ers, the 'there go I but for the grace of God'-ers and the 'why doesn't someone just put them out of their misery'-ers. Roughly translated, this meant he could be of immense help to me in a) getting to grips with the festival and b) getting me into parties. It also meant he was well aware of all the pitfalls that a Festival novice like myself could easily fall into. He was very helpful and we rehearsed till the Mingers showed up with a loud Liverpudlian flurry of 'Cooeee, only us, Edinburgh here we come . . . this is mental, innit . . . like . . . like . . . mint!'

The Mingers physically lived up to their stage name. In comedy terms they were mongrels, I'd venture related to the Staffordshire bull terrier breed: biting humour and rough with it. They turned to me, hoop earrings, hair pulled back, lip liner prominent and said, 'So Brodsky, what exactly did you do to convince Gerry to give you a place in the show?' Their tone full of innuendo.

'That would be telling,' I replied, caught offguard by their directness.

'Go on, we're listening.' Arms crossed, they expected a reply.

'Nothing. She called and offered me a spot.'

'So why you blushing? Are you a carpet-muncher?' They both laughed raucously. 'Look at her face,' and then further mocked my reaction. 'Don't worry luv, we won't tell Lisa.'

'Won't tell Lisa what?' Lisa appeared round the bar door and purred in a low, sexy voice, 'Hello there and how are we all?'

DROP-DEAD GORGEOUS

It was the first time I'd seen Lisa since the abysmal competition show. She defied comedy classification. Lisa was a freckle-faced twenty-six-year-old, with rose-bud pink lips and a mop of strawberry-blonde curls bobbing shoulder-length on a petite, perfect body. The Baby Spice of comedy, but clever. There wasn't a canine bone in her body. From where I was standing, she had it all. I stood further back. Yep, she definitely had it all.

Over the next half-hour I didn't get a word in,

merely observed as Lisa, Adrian and the Mingers quickly caught up on all the gossip and news over tea and biscuits. Then we started discussing the running order of the show and who would go on first.

FIRST ON

The position of first on was not a popular one in any comedy line-up. Basically it's the short straw. The audience may not be sufficiently warmed up, aka drunk enough, so if up first, you had to work harder to get the audience on side. Should you storm it, it set a standard for the rest of the evening. The audience relaxed and usually enjoyed the remainder of the show. Then again, the first act could often be regarded as the sacrificial lamb and if it was spit-roasted by the audience, the following acts were often treated less harshly. It's a win-win situation for everyone but the comic who got to go on first. We decided to pull straws. Four were pulled and although all of equal length, mine was perceived by Lisa, Adrian and the Mingers as dwarfish. The unanimous decision was taken that I would go on first, every night, for the entire run. I objected, to no avail – my position was firmly fixed. It was official; I was the runt of the pack.

'Good to see you settling in so well,' observed Geraldine, who had watched the show and given notes at the end of it. We were enjoying a post-preview drink in the bar below. I was chuffed, glad there had been no major hiccups.

'Issy?' Lisa tapped me on the shoulder. 'I wanted to say something.' She focused her intensely blue eyes on me. 'I wanted to say . . . okay, I'm going to spit it out, even if it makes me seem strange. Issy, remember the night of the competition?'

'Huh?'

'The night of the competition. Remember?'

I nodded. How could I forget? My face immediately took on the shame position, the hangdog downward nod.

'Remember when you ran up on stage to get the prize . . .'

'I swear on my mother's life I thought my name had been called out. Lisa/Issy, they are both sibilant.'

'I could see how devastated you were.'

Understatement. I nodded again, my chin hitting my chest.

'You must have really hated me. If I was you, I'd have really hated me.'

It had to be said, she was very perceptive. Upon pain of death I had sworn her my lifelong enemy. Yes, I was jealous. Yes, I did resent her talent, looks, the whole package, though personally I meant her no harm.

'Lisa, that was one of the worst moments in my life.'

She leaned back in horror. 'Only *one* of the worst?'

'Let's not go there.'

81

'The thing is, Issy, I don't want any bad feelings to stew between us. This show is really important to me.'

'It's really important to me, too.'

'Good. Friends?' She waved a white paper napkin at me. My overriding intention being to befriend her, I gladly took her up on the offer.

'Sure, best of,' I replied.

FULL STEAM AHEAD

We'd hit July at full speed and were almost halfway through. I was frantically trying to organise myself and ended up forgoing adult rationale and reverting to childhood antics to get what was required. Not as in throwing tantrums; instead I played my parents off one another like back in the good old days. It seemed to be working. They were responding favourably, so much so it became an 'access to' argument. Max was in high demand. My mum had finally confirmed she could do the last two weeks of August.

'That sounds fine, Mum, more than fine, it sounds amazing. I promise, I won't let you down, you're going to be so proud of me and . . .'

'Darling, you've got to sort out your approval-seeking issues.'

'Mother, I'm a comedian, it's part and parcel of the trade.'

Next up was my father.

'Guess what? My most amazing mother, your ex-first wife, has just pledged to look after Max for the last couple of weeks in August . . .'

'Really? And will she be with that twit of a partner of hers?'

'It's not his fault his name is Wally.'

'He could have changed it by deed poll.'

The last time my parents had met was at Max's Welcome to the World birthday party. Each came accompanied by their respective partner. It was the worst party I'd been to, never mind thrown. Max was just ten days old, he wailed all day, my nipples were aching, down below not much better and, to cap it off, my brother Freddie decided it was an apt moment to come out. My father immediately blamed my mother, who was all for taking it as a compliment, but Wally decided to come to her defence. A meek man by nature, his stature went against him, being six-four and built like a house. He made my father (five-foot-eleven in a good pair of hidden-heel shoes) very, very uncomfortable and the situation deteriorated into a stand-off in my living room.

'As long as Wally isn't on English soil, I'd be more than happy to come.'

I'd already cross-checked with my mother. Apparently he was going on an expedition down the Amazon.

'So do you think you'll be able to help, Dad?' I asked again.

'Of course, but those last two weeks were the ones I wanted . . .'

Agh, I knew my father well. We shared a similar trait of always wanting what we couldn't have.

'Mum is fairly adaptable. I'm sure she won't mind swapping.' I called him back half an hour later. 'Yeah, that's no problem, she'll swap.'

'Super, that's all worked out perfectly then. Can't wait to see Maxy, and how is your mum? How's she looking?'

My father was officially back on the market and in hunting mode, although the reason both his previous marriages failed was that he had never really taken himself out of the market.

'Mum is looking great. I'm not sure about the dreadlocks.'

He groaned.

'Neither is she,' I confided. 'She said she was thinking of shaving her head for the summer.'

He groaned again then added, 'Great, I won't feel so self-conscious about my bald pate.'

And that was how I overcame all my Obligations, Responsibilities and Duties on the road to Edinburgh.

HOT BLUE-COLLAR WORK

It was a ridiculously hot day in the office and temperatures were running high. To make matters worse, the atmosphere was heavy with Fiona's affected premenstrual tension.

I was having a verbal spat with Lady A, who had turned against me with a vengeance. I'd only called to advertise our special summer sizzler offer – buy two hours of surveillance and receive one free. How was I supposed to know it was meant to have been the day of Her Ladyship's nuptials? I found her in a very emotional state, grieving her phantom wedding.

'I was meant to be getting married today . . .' she howled and then, between sobs, acquainted me with the pitiful tale of how Henry had unceremoniously dumped her after having fallen in 'true love' with one of the strippers. I was shocked, appalled and rapt.

'I don't believe it!' I gasped in my best Victor Meldrew.

'Issy, you promised me absolutely nothing untoward had happened.'

'I can assure you nothing did, not in my presence,' I responded on the defensive.

'I have evidence,' she declared, 'and I have a witness. The best man will testify.'

Her distress transformed into vicious hatred toward me.

'There is the small matter of a matchbox I found from the club with the whore's telephone number scrawled on it.'

'Look Lady, I was there till the mass arrest. There was no cavorting, never mind fraternising with the employees.'

'I find that hard to believe. The tramp wrote, "Light

me up big boy and give me call." I repeat, I have the box of matches.'

'Impossible . . .' I replied, but then recalled the act prior to mine, the one with the peculiar smoking habit. I vaguely remembered the performer asking Henry if he wouldn't mind lighting up her cigarette. She handed him the box of matches and thus began her act.

'Listen Araminta, there's no way I can be held responsible for that, but if you are so determined to get your man back, maybe you should take up the habit.'

'Or maybe I should just sue you,' she snidely suggested.

In response I advised her in a most patronising tone that I'd pretend she hadn't said that and we would put her silly, nonsensical notion down to a rejected and shattered heart. I heard her nostrils flare and then she broke down once more and fell into ear-piercing wails of 'woe is me'.

I did feel for Her Ladyship, but not much. Okay, so she was incredibly depressed and a smidge crazy, but the fact remained that she was loaded. She owned a substantial piece of northern England. She was a catch; she'd find a replacement for her Hooray Henry soon enough. I slammed the phone down and then thrust my sweaty face as close to the crappy desk fan as possible.

Fiona was avidly filing. This was her way of dealing with frustration. Geraldine had called earlier to cancel a dinner arrangement and thus cemented Fiona's foul mood. She was vying for a fight, kept harassing me about Lisa Slater.

'Anything to report yet? Have you gained access to her inner sanctum?'

'No! Give me a break, Fiona.'

'No slacking. I want results, Brodsky.'

'Don't worry, you'll have results.'

'And what's happening with the money owed by Penn?' Trisha butted in.

'I can't seem to get hold of him,' I replied honestly.

'Brodsky, you should never have worked those hours until the money was in.'

My cheeks turned puce. Pay at the Trap was based on commission. I was going to have to do something and soon: either pay up, own up or make up a very good excuse.

'Seeing as you're pissing off on a Highland mission,' Trisha continued and I noted that she threw up her eyes as she said this, 'I'll give Nadia that case.'

'You sure?' and I thought in the circumstances that was a smart idea.

'Positive. Make certain you give me your notes before you leave though.'

'Eh, okay,' and I made a note to write some.

Meanwhile, Nads was puking up in the toilets. Morning sickness had kicked in, though in her case it carried on well into the day. For four days running she'd blamed her dodgy stomach on bad curries. Trisha was getting suspicious.

'If she's brought E. coli into this office . . .' she muttered.

I volunteered to go and check up on her. And it was while she leaned over the porcelain and I rubbed her back that I told her about the Arthur Penn case. Everything there was to know, except the money bit, and I begged her to help me. She branded me an idiot.

'Brodsky, you're too much. An undercover agent losing their own client,' and she heaved some more.

We struck a deal. In return for Nadia's help I promised not to reveal her pregnancy to Trisha or Fiona (it was only a few more weeks until Nadia qualified for full maternity benefits), not bitch about Kassie being chief bridesmaid and also to undertake and organise the hen party. We shook on it, our friendship re-ignited in our mutual complicity.

'Issy, I haven't said this, but make the most of Edinburgh. These opportunities only come once in a while.'

'Thanks Nads,' I answered. 'Do you think I'm going to be really famous?'

Her response unfortunately was not easily translated into the vernacular.

THE STARS OF TOMORROW, TODAY!

Tonight, live on stage in Islington . . . .

Our final London preview before Edinburgh. The crowd were fairly responsive, consisting solely of

88

friends and family. My brother Freddie came with his surgeon boyfriend. It was so unfair to think he pulled much better-looking guys than I ever did. This one was gorgeous, a real beauty and charming with it. I told him he could operate on me any day.

'Actually,' he replied, 'you could do with a bit of a lift . . .'

'Danny is a cosmetic surgeon,' my brother smiled awkwardly.

'Marry the man now,' I whispered to Freddie, before slipping into my costume, ready for my imminent performance.

Again, the show went well enough. We had a few post-preview drinks, then disbanded into the night. Lisa and I were standing at the bus stop dissecting our performances joke by joke – or, rather, mine.

'Issy, that joke is definitely your weakest,' Lisa advised. 'Drop it.'

'Really? I nearly always get a laugh. I thought it was quite strong.'

'It's too naff. It's a groaner rather than a laugh.'

I bowed to her better judgment. For years I'd thought stand-up comedians were spontaneous raconteurs and that jokes were made on the spur of the moment. However, most comedians have scripted sets that they reel off, though the more experienced they become, the easier it is to freestyle. My present level was strictly scripted and then fine-tooth-combed. Standing at the bus stop Lisa purged my set of three knob gags and one cancer joke. The latter I protested about, but she was adamant and felt it was in bad taste. I argued the whole set was in bad taste, but relinquished the joke nonetheless. Rubbing her up the wrong way was not in my interest.

'Guess you'll miss Geraldine?' I supposed, trying to change the topic before any more of my material went in for the chop.

'Expect so,' she replied, nonplussed.

'Sorry to hear about her going into hospital.'

'How did you know?'

I was stumped. 'Was I not supposed to know?'

'She was hoping to keep it quiet.'

'How come it's all so hush-hush? What is wrong with her?'

'Lady-of-a-certain-age stuff.'

'Sorry, I'm being nosy, you don't have to tell me.'

'One of the pitfalls of smoking,' she replied with a wink.

Oh shit! Cancer. Geraldine was a heavy smoker, not to mention imbiber. No wonder Lisa had axed my cancer joke from the show.

Just then we heard shrieking and all eyes turned to a little woman across the road, leaping up and down excitedly.

'Lief,' she cried out, pointing at me. 'Lief!'

I chose to ignore her.

'Lady lief . . .'

It was Won Ton Lily, the cleaning lady from the house next door to Arthur Penn's house, which wasn't really Arthur Penn's house at all, who had bumped into me running out of it the day I had gone over there to give it the once-over. Fact was, I hadn't even taken anything. Damn, but I hated being unjustly accused.

'Who the hell is she?' Lisa asked.

'No idea,' I squirmed uncomfortably.

'She's pointing at you.'

'No she isn't.'

'She is, Issy.'

Christ, all I needed was this hysterical madwoman giving me grief. Won Ton Lily was attempting to cross the street. 'You lady lief, bad lady, get police . . .'

The traffic lights turned in my favour, the volume of traffic sufficient to keep her at bay, and then the timely arrival of a night bus, though not the right bus.

'Lisa, I'm off, see you up in Edinburgh,' I spluttered, climbing on board and praying the bus driver was one of those types who, when spotting in their side mirror someone running for their bus usually drove off all the faster. The side-view mirror reflected Won Ton Lily sprinting toward the stop. I glanced at the driver and thought: please, please react to type . . . She was gaining ground, mere metres from the open door when he sneered in that smug 'hate all passengers' manner, then released his clutch. We were off.

*   *   *

91

Forty-eight hours from Edinburgh. The finer details had all been smoothed over. I had an apartment lined up, a case to follow, a decent ten-minute set and sufficient child cover. What could possibly go wrong?

'I HATE YOU!'

Max screamed and then, just in case not everyone had heard, shouted, 'I really, really hate you, Mum.'

'Jeez Max, I'm sorry. I promise I'll never call you Maxikins in public again.'

This was our last day together before Edinburgh and I'd envisaged it as being one of complete togetherness, tenderness and full of love. Not a boy of five going on fifteen, red in the face with anger and howling at me. I understood he felt humiliated. I reached out to kiss him and made matters ten times worse. We were at the swimming pool in Archway, acoustically speaking not in my favour.

'I want to go to the wave pool,' Max had decided earlier that morning when asked what he would like to do. So up we went. School had finished the week before and he was delighted to bump into some of his friends. Already I was a last-resort playmate but hey, that's par for the course.

'You are the worst mum in the world!' he bawled.

By this stage people were watching. My parenting skills were being put to the test. Aware that the last few months had been emotionally intense for Max, I had no doubt the forthcoming one would be, too.

'Max, I'm sorry. I promise I'll never call you that again.' I pleaded with him to calm down.

'I hate you. It's all your fault,' he raged. We had to get out of the pool pronto, as his friends had started pointing at him, which sent his sense of distress soaring higher. Hoping we wouldn't slip on the wet surface, I dragged him through to the changing area, then, forgoing the shower, wrapped him tightly in a towel.

'Max, I love you. I am so sorry. I really am,' I intoned, holding him tight till the shouts turned to sobs and I rocked him in my arms like when he was a baby.

OUR LAST SUPPER — WELL, LUNCH

We left the earlier episode back in the changing rooms and went to our favourite place, Marine Ices, to stuff our faces on pizza. Waiting to be served, I prayed Max wasn't going to throw another wobbly.

'You're going to have such a good time with Granny and Gramps.'

'Maybe,' he replied.

'For sure you will.' I pushed a gift-wrapped box across the table and his eyes lit up. He ripped the paper off with enthusiastic force and inside lay a game for his PlayStation.

'Wicked!' he declared as if catapulted to kid nirvana. 'You're the best mum ever.'

Lunch over, we decided to climb to the top of Primrose Hill, our hands clasped round heavy cones of ice-cream. It was a sweet ascent to the summit. We sat in silence enjoying the view. Every so often it seems to me that we two are synchronised, tuned to perfection.

My father had fondly recounted Max's reaction over how he'd cope without me. 'So do you think you'll be okay?' he'd asked Max during one of their phone conversations.

'Yeah, but I'm not sure about Mum.'

'What do you mean?' asked my dad.

'I think she'll really miss me.'

We played Kick Rock on the homeward journey, the object of the game being simple but effective: to kick a stone all the way back to the apartment. Max won. After I put him to bed, I wrote three letters for 'emergency missing-Mummy moments', wrapped up a couple more surprise presents, another game for his PlayStation, a couple of books, puzzles and a treasure box full of sweets.

READY OR NOT

'You all packed?' My mum's shaven head poked round the door of my room. She'd already made herself at home, having hung up her windchimes and laid out the meditation mat.

'Yeah, just about.'

'How do you feel?'

'Shit scared,' I replied.

FINAL PARTING WORDS

Me to Trisha:

'What do you mean you didn't get the notes on Arthur Penn?' *Detecting: A Way of Life*, Rule Number 248, Article D, Subsection II: Always act dumb.

'There's no notes here.' Trisha sounded peeved.

'I emailed them to you yesterday,' I protested.

'They're not here and I can't find them on your computer. You did print out a hard copy, didn't you?'

'Oh no . . .'

'What?'

'I have a really bad feeling.'

'What, Brodsky?'

'Massive computer crash yesterday, just my luck the files will have suffered.'

'What do you mean suffered?'

'You know, deletion.'

'Oh for God's sake . . .'

'Anyhow, must dash, have a plane to catch.'

'Brodsky!'

'Gotta go, don't you know.'

'Brodsky!'

'Must run, have fun.'

'Brodsky!'

'Oh damn, you're breaking up.'

Me to my dad:

'What do you mean, you're on your way over?'

'I told you, I was coming for the first two weeks.'

'No Dad, you specifically requested the last two weeks.'

'It's too late to change my plans now.'

'Dad!'

Me to Nads:

'You won't believe this Nads . . .'

'Issy, you won't believe this either.'

'What?'

'Arthur Penn didn't die.'

'What do you mean?'

'He didn't just pass away.'

'What do you mean?'

'His heart didn't just seize up and it was bye-bye world, hello heaven.'

'What do you mean?'

'Issy, this is quite a peculiar case.'

'What do you mean?'

'There's more to this case than meets the eye.'

'Get to the point, Nadia!'

'Arthur Penn was murdered.'

'Oh my God, so you mean . . . I really was following a ghost.'

'A ghost?'

And all this before 10am. Next up . . .

Me to Scarface through his letterbox:
'Open up, Scarface! I've come to say goodbye. Look, about the other night, it was really stupid of me and . . .'

I knew he was in from the amount of noise he'd made the night before.

'Hey Scarface, I know you're in there. Come out, come out or I'll huff and I'll puff . . .'

'Coming.' He didn't sound too pleased, or that hung over. Then I heard a giggle. A giggle belonging to a member of the female gender. 'This is a bad time, Issy.'

'Yeah, obviously.' Tears started streaming down my cheeks. 'Shit. I just thought you'd like to wish me good luck.'

'Sorry Issy, I . . .'

'It's over, Scarface. O.V.E.R.'

For the first time in our relationship I felt total hatred toward Scarface. Okay, so maybe not for the first time. It was just that now I could put a name to the feeling. He was such an arrogant, self-centred man whose real name was Derek and not Scarface at all. I'd never much liked the name, hence the nickname. Put side by side our names didn't seem to hang well. I should have taken it as an omen right from the start.

Me to my mother:
'I can't believe I was so stupid.'

She tried out some more healing on me. 'It's okay, Issy, let it out, it's fine.'

Blubber, blubber till I reached a decent state of mental recovery and Terminal One at Heathrow.

'I'm trusting you with Max's life. His life. I swear to God, Mum, if anything happens, if anything happens . . .'

'Issy, stop it.'

'Okay, sorry. Oh yeah, I forgot to tell you – Dad is coming over tomorrow.'

'I thought he was doing the last two weeks.'

'So did I.'

'Issy.' My mother's eyes narrowed. 'When did you find out?'

'A couple of hours ago. Believe me, Mum, I had no idea and I may as well warn you, I think he's in one of his moods.'

'What do you mean?'

'Randy.'

'Oh for God's sake . . .'

Me to the main man:
'Max, I'm going to call you every day, write letters to you. I love you so, so, so, so much . . .' A torrent of kisses rained down on him and I suppressed the urge to run away with my own child. 'Maxers, have the best time ever.'

'You too, Mum.' He was holding my mother's

hand and blowing kisses to me while I walked backwards in the general direction of the departure lounge. It was all very romantic until I hit a wall.

Me to Fiona:
'Fiona, what's up? My flight has just been called.'

'Merely checking up on you, don't want you forgetting you have a mission to accomplish.' Her voice was terse and officious.

'Affirmative.'

''Cause I'll be keeping tabs.'

'Okay.'

'I want hard evidence, got it? Salacious dirt. Proper notes, Brodsky.'

'I'm reading you, boss, loud and clear.'

I suspected Trisha must have said something.

Row twelve, window seat. Having boarded the plane I turned off my mobile, fastened my seatbelt and contemplated the spiritual. Well, when sky-bound one's thoughts tend to turn celestial.

Me to God:
Hey Old Man, it's finally beginning to happen for me. My moment has come. The opportunity I've chased for so long, like a balloon afloat finally within my grasp. Lord, I'm feeling so excited, apprehensive, nervous, anxious . . . Christ, I think I'm about to have a panic attack.

In an emergency, press the overhead button for attention.

Me to hostess:
'Can I have a glass of water please?'
  'Are you okay?'
  'A bit of a panic attack.'
  'Would you like some oxygen?'
  'You wouldn't have a Valium?'
  'No.' But the mother with the three screaming kids further down the aisle did.

Sorry about that, G, where were we?
God, I sure hope I'm doing the right thing. There's this feeling in the pit of my belly I can only describe as a teeny, bolshy American baseball trainer, jumping up and down, hooting and screaming, 'You can do it, you can do it,' punching his own palm with excitement. He's so enthusiastic and for a moment I believe it. Yeah, I can do it. Go for it. Then suddenly there's this lady, terribly well groomed with great legs and she's gazing at me with disdain, looking down her nose at me – she doesn't even have to say a thing. I know exactly what she's thinking from her expression. God, I'm scared. I am so very scared of failing, of letting everyone down, of what people will think of me, of being one of the few thirty-recurring people performing at the fringe, of everyone being ten years younger than me and childless, of Max suffering due to my selfishness, of the evolving spooky case of Arthur

Penn, of not collating the evidence required for Fiona to expose Lisa. Of never getting the chance to fall in love again, or always falling for the same old bastards. (I know the last two fears aren't directly connected to Edinburgh, just thought I'd purge myself of the lot of them.) Oh yeah, and lastly, of not being funny.

The seatbelt lights were flashing.

Our descent into Edinburgh had begun.

God, here goes everything and hey, I'm trusting you are keeping an eye on me from up there.

And finally:
'See you on the other side.'

Me, to myself, catching sight of my reflection in the aeroplane window. Which in retrospect turned out to be incredibly prescient.

LIVING THE DREAM

This Athens of the north
A walkers' paradise
Her beauty
Shrouded in a sea mist, Har
As if the heavens lapped street-level
How apt then the circumstance
For setting free dreams
Tread softly.[1]

FIRST IMPRESSIONS

The cabby took the scenic route from the airport to a
residential street just north of the Meadows, a park area
lying south of the castle, which dominates the city landscape, all of which is an architectural visual treat, with an
old town–new town divide, and can inspire even the most
non-poetic person to verse. (Ahem, ahem, see above.)

Index finger pressing down on Flat 8, 62 Lemming

---

1 Big shout out to my main man, Yeats, though if I was really clever it
would have been Burns.

Terrace, I inhaled a deep breath of the unknown. Set free from my little anchorman, it occurred to one that I, as newcomer in this world of comedy, could be anyone. For an entire month I would be childless, responsible only for myself. Hypothetically I could stay out all night, sleep all day and do exactly as I wanted. Of course, I had the nightly show and to keep a private eye on Lisa but, having come from the constraints of mummydom, it felt liberating, exhilarating, unnerving. I was freefalling without parachute, safety net, landing pad, ground even. I was by then hauling my luggage up four flights of stone stairs with Adrian huffing and puffing in front of me. I'd envisaged the apartment as similar to the one in the film *Shallow Grave*, ie, large, funky, high-ceilinged rooms with wood floors throughout. Unfortunately I had to deflate these expectations. Once over the threshold we passed through decades and entered a dwelling firmly entrenched in the 1980s, that period being the last time the property was cleaned, never mind refurbished. The smell of filth was all-pervasive.

'You okay?' asked Adrian.

My cavernous jaw and horror-struck eyes must have subtly hinted at my given mind-set. I nodded dumbly in shock. The place was a dump. I had not been in an environment like this since my student days.

'Not bad, eh?' Adrian grinned. He showed me around. One of the bedrooms had no windows, the kitchen had no door. The décor was a mish-mash of hideousness: purple walls, peeling paper, woodchip, threadbare carpet, cork floor-tiles well worn through.

Though scuzzy, it was at least large. There were four bedrooms, the remaining two waiting to be filled by the Mingers and Lisa. The former touched down with a raucous cheer of, 'Oh my God . . . like . . . Jesus . . . this place is rank, mingin' like . . .'

Lisa arrived shortly after and once again straws were pulled, only this time for the rooms. Metaphorically, of course, as Lisa deemed that rooms should be allotted in accordance with comedy experience. So Adrian got the huge room, Lisa the bright room, the Mingers the room with a view and I got the one without the window, ie, the cell.

'HOW IS IT, DARLING?'

The first night spent, the bed bugs' war commenced, the early-morning trip to Argos to get a blow-up mattress undertaken, and the small fortune for household detergents exchanged. I wanted to cry, but told my father everything was okay and demanded to speak to Max, whether he wanted to or not, never mind that he was watching cartoons and had to be dragged away.

'Hi Mum,' he groaned, annoyed I'd disturbed his viewing pleasure.

'How's it going, Maxy?'

'Good, I'm going horse riding today.'

'No way!'

'For real, Mum.'

Placated by his joy, I let his words soothe me, centre me and I told him about my awful room and the castle on the hill and the mountain in the shape of a seat.

'Mum, d'you wanna speak to Grandma now?' This was Max's way of ending the conversation and me realising all was fine. Before I had a chance to reply he'd passed over the receiver. My mother was less enthusiastic, as father's arrival had somewhat thrown her emotional equilibrium askance.

'Rationally, Issy, I know it's not your fault, but I feel that indirectly it is.'

'Mother,' I pressed her, 'how could that possibly be?'

'Your father said you changed the dates, or something about the dates and you . . .'

'Mum, I swear on your life, this was all of Dad's contriving.'

'Well, we were joking last night that you were attempting to bring us back together.'

'Oh pur-lease. As if. Actually, how are you two getting on?'

'MORE THAN WELL – I'D SAY WE WERE HITTING IT OFF . . .'

'Fiona, it's early days, but really you don't have to check up on me the whole time.'

'Remember, Issy, I'm the client and as such the client is always . . .'

'Right, speak to you later.' I'd spotted Lisa walking into the crowded café and was enthusiastically waving at her.

Having spent the morning scrubbing my cell, I fled the chemically infused flat to the safety of Café Blunt and was flicking through the events programme. The first thing to strike home was the scale of the Edinburgh Festival. To be succinct, it's the daddy of all arts festivals, incorporating film, theatre, fringe, comedy, books, opera, jazz, blues, pop and dance. Try to imagine London and a large percentage of the international arts community descending on a city for a month to showcase their wares and, well, that's Edinburgh in August. There are literally thousands of shows running twenty-four hours a day in hundreds of places. It had taken me two large cappuccinos to work out that the main Fringe venues were the Assembly Rooms, the Pleasance and the Gilded Balloon, though they were merely blanket terms covering loads of different spaces. It was completely overwhelming, mesmerising and totally flabbergasting.

I sat meekly sipping my coffee, paralysed by choice and filling in the time before our first technical run. Lisa plonked herself down beside me. Scrubbed of make-up she looked ridiculously fresh faced and apple-blossom pretty, 'Found any interesting shows?' she enquired.

'I'm overawed by the choice.'

'Don't worry, you'll soon . . .' her mobile interrupted our burgeoning conversation. 'Hello, my darling,' she

106

cooed, overly affectionate. 'Yes I remember. Yes, we're doing a technical run today. Don't worry. Yes, Adrian is picking up the boxes of flyers. Yes, and the posters. You are such an old fusspot.' Her tone was nauseously endearing and she was giggling. 'Stop it. Issy is staring at me like I have two heads . . . Okay. I promise, love you.' The conversation ended and abruptly Lisa switched attitude. 'Geraldine is so insecure,' she remarked, then asked, 'Are you with anyone, Issy?'

I enlightened Lisa as to the whys and wherefores of my single status, spilled my soul on to the table, and told her the whole sorry Scarface saga from A–Z.

'What a complete tosser,' she replied frankly. 'Don't worry, you'll have a lot of fun here. Edinburgh is a shagfest.'

'Seriously?'

'Even the Mingers'll get lucky, it's guaranteed.'

In consideration of my openness, I hoped Lisa would reciprocate.

'You and Geraldine seem really in love,' began my opening gambit. I wanted to try to work out where Lisa was coming from and how much she was in love with Geraldine.

'Do we?' she considered.

Guess I was going to have to try harder. 'Been together long?'

'Not very.'

I wondered who wore the pants in their relationship and what sort of pants they were. I returned her bluntness with some of my own.

'Have you always been a lesbian?'

'Why, do you fancy me?' jested Lisa. She was giving me the Look. You know the one, the 'come hither', 'green light', 'you're on to a winner', 'the night is full of promise', 'seduce me now, big boy' look. I remembered it well – used to give it to guys in my former heyday.

'God, no,' I yelped way too shrilly, drawing attention from the table beside us. 'I'm not that way inclined.'

'Have you ever tried it?'

'Never,' I protested. As far as I was concerned there's a big difference between general lady-pant curiosity and trying to get into someone's.

'Issy, maybe you should broaden your horizons?' She was teasing me and it was working. If I'd been wearing a collar I surely would have been hot beneath it.

'I like my horizons just how they are, thanks,' I said.

'You're scared, you're in denial.'

'Listen, Lisa, try as hard as you like, I shan't succumb.' She raised her eyes at me, so for good measure I added, 'That's not a challenge.'

'We'll see,' she replied and, taking me by the hand, she led me over to our venue, the Caves, for our first technical run.

'When Geraldine said the Caves, I . . .'

'Didn't believe her?' Adrian staggered in, weighed down with boxes of posters. It hadn't seemed important to me where I would be performing, only that I would be performing. The Caves II, Cowgate, was part of Edinburgh's underground city, where it was said that

108

in times past the healthy citizens of Edinburgh left the disease-ridden to fester and die a cruel, agonising death.

'When did this all happen?' I asked.

'Centuries back. Don't worry, the worst you'll suffer these days is a bout of bronchitis.'

Our cave lived up to its name, a dark, dank, dripping venue, where at the eleventh hour of every evening for the forthcoming month we would strike up the Late Night Titter Club.

'THE TIT-WHAT?'

'An hour-long, rip-roaring, hilarious, late-night comedy show,' I explained to the ACTOR standing beside me. My Festival initiation in full flow, I was out pasting up posters. The entire city was wallpapered with them, space at a premium. We would have come to blows if he hadn't been gorgeous, dripping with charm and had a terribly commanding ACTOR'S voice.

'Are you an ACTOR?' I asked. (Hey, with that tosser Scarface out of the picture, it was time to move on, I was a single mo . . . I mean single again.)

'I am. And you?'

'A stand-up comedienne,' I modestly replied. 'What show are you in?'

'An avant-garde improvisational show. Every night a unique performance.'

I was impressed, as I hadn't a clue what he meant.

'Who's she?' He indicated the eye-catching vision of Lisa licking a lolly, with a star-shaped picture of a Minger tastefully placed, one on each breast.

'She's our star attraction.'

'Great cleavage. Any good?'

'Not for you.'

'Excuse me?'

'I meant, she's a lesbian.'

'Ah. I meant is she a good performer?'

Three hours later I was back at the flat, last in line for the trickle of water that had the audacity to label itself a shower. We were getting ready for the grand opening party of the festival. Fiona called again and this time berated me for not having recorded the flirtatious conversation earlier in the café.

'Remember, whatever it takes, Issy.'

'Fiona,' I mumbled, 'I'll do whatever it takes, but I won't do that.'

'Listen clearly, dipstick,' Fiona continued, 'I want enough evidence so Geraldine realises she's being made a complete ass of.'

'How is Geraldine?' I asked.

'Under the knife as we speak . . .'

I was thinking along the lines of some type of -ectomy, hyster-, mast-. 'Ouch. Poor thing. I hope she pulls through.'

'There's no reason why she shouldn't. It's pretty routine these days.'

Then, from the corner of my eye and left nostril, I

saw and smelt a noxiously perfumed Minger emerge from the steamy bathroom. I cut the conversation short, promising Fiona I'd keep an extra-vigilant eye on Lisa at the party.

'WHAT DO YOU MEAN, SHE'S DISAPPEARED?'

One minute she was there and the next . . .

I suppose I should have stayed sober but we 'Titters' had some serious bonding to do, and how better to do it than over a bottle of tequila?

Kitted out with our requisite passes proclaiming us 'artistes', high heels donned and cheeks rouged, we girls meandered toward the Gilded Balloon up at Bristo Square to the official opening party. Then, swanking past security and into the dining room, we found the place was already a-throng with performers, press, producers, basically anyone and everyone involved in the Festival. It was clearly time to . . .

P.A.R.T.Y.

Drink one: my throat opened.
  Drink two: my tongue started wagging.
  Drink three: we Tits got high-speed verbal.

Drink four: we shared childhood stories.

Drink five: then sexual escapades.

Drink six: intimate secrets. 'And,' I proclaimed self-righteously and probably a little too loudly, 'I could hear her in Scarface's flat giggling. Jesus, what a bastard. I declare him history! On to bigger (I mean that in every possible way) and better.'

Lisa yawned forcefully, having heard it all before. 'Oops. No disrespect, Issy, but it's really not that interesting . . .'

Drink seven: we toasted ourselves. 'Great Tits, friends for ever, friends for life,' then immediately disbanded, agreeing to set forth and mingle. Our first undertaking was to go on a recce and draw up wish-lists of heavenly male or female comedians that we Tits would most like to do or be done to.

PADDY ENGLISHMAN, PADDY IRISHMAN AND PADDY SCOTSMAN

The bar was overflowing with comedians of all sorts. The English ones were most easily typified by class, the upper being twattish/surreal. Then came the aficionados of smart-arse comedy, otherwise known as the middle class – 'I'm so very clever with my Oxbridge education and TV/radio contact' (BBC, natch, including the ethnic minorities, who were all the rage). Next come the neurotic apologists with degrees from more provincial universities or ex-polytechnics, then the working class, speaking directly to the people in an all-inclusive ITV way. Women comedians had a tendency to be classified in, surprise, surprise, more physical terms: fat-funny, ugly-funny, or, and this was the option I preferred, character actress. Where was I in the scheme of things? I was with Lisa, sitting in the gallery peering down to the bar below.

'Women are so much more beautiful then men, don't you think, Issy?'

'Maybe, but men have dicks.' I had been hoping she was going to drop the lesbo stuff, as it was beginning to make me feel uncomfortable.

'I can't believe you've never kissed another woman.'

'Vice versa.'

'You're so naïve. I'm bisexual.'

'Oh my God,' I declared, mouth gaping in shock, 'I don't believe it . . .'

'Most people are, they just don't acknowledge that side of their sexuality.'

'Whatever . . .' My tongue was lolling, for I'd just glimpsed Jake Vincent. Yes, *the* Jake Vincent, the gorgeous US actor, last seen in that brilliant independent movie he wrote and directed.

'See that guy, Lisa?' I pointed to him.

'Who? Jake Vincent?'

'Yeah,' I smiled. 'What's he doing here?'

'I think he's involved in one of the theatre productions.' I couldn't believe she was so blasé about this star descending to the low level of our pleb presence.

'Oh my God, I have to meet him. He is so sexy. He's my number-one choice,' I jubilantly declared.

Lisa laughed, 'Issy, he's way out of your league.'

MY NUMBER-ONE CHOICE

A description of Jake Vincent to merit his visual magnificence: he was touching six foot, broad shouldered and with a wide chest you could drum your tiny little clenched fists against in bouts of Vivien Leigh versus Clark Gable. He had a wide smile and lush lips, green eyes, tanned skin, a mixture of intense manliness and utter vulnerability, a huge amount of talent and (I looked and looked) no obvious signs of a girlfriend.

I leaned against the gallery, emitting sonar love signals to no avail. Lisa elbowed me in the ribs. 'Forget it.'

'There's no harm in looking, Lisa. Now as for this guy . . .' I clocked the ACTOR I'd met earlier in the day while out pasting posters, and he was making his way straight toward us.

'ISSY BRODSKY! AND WHAT EXACTLY ARE YOU DOING HERE?'

At the bar, I was squashed in between Jake V and another sycophantic fan eager to rub shoulders. My

114

round just happened to coincide with his. How convenient. I mad-dashed it to the bar, leaving the ACTOR with Lisa. Playing it cool, I made out like it was no big deal to be standing right up next to Jake Vincent and, my confidence bolstered by far too much alcohol, I felt obliged to introduce myself. Then I made a joke. He laughed. Unbelievably, I made another humorous remark and he laughed again. I was going to go for a third, but caught sight of Lisa and the ACTOR.

'And where did you say your show was on?'

Damn, damn, Jake Vincent was interested in having a conversation with me and Lisa was whispering something to the ACTOR.

'Caves II.'

'What time?'

'Huh? 11pm.' The ACTOR had draped his arm around Lisa's waist.

'Too bad, we clash. My show's on the same time. Maybe we could . . .'

'Oh . . . shit.' The ACTOR and Lisa were making their way toward the exit. 'Sorry, Jake, I've got to go.' I ran back up to the gallery, only to be ambushed by the Mingers. They threw their arms around me and claimed me for themselves. 'Issy, you slag . . . how's about you?'

Me?

Well, I was drunk. So very pissed . . . off. The first night and I'd managed to lose Lisa. I cursed myself, cursed Lisa, the Mingers, the ACTOR, Fiona, even Geraldine. I was on a roll, so added Scarface, threw in Arthur, whoever the hell he turned out to be, but mostly I damned my lifelong capacity for losing things like the finger (see previous opus), my jobs, men, Arthur . . . and now Lisa.

THE MORNING AFTER

I woke with my short-term memory slightly pickled. Events of the previous night flashed through my mind like Gareth Gates's stammer. I . . . I . . . I . . . had:

a) a good time?
b) a very good time?
c) messed up?
d) an ominous feeling the answer was going to be c.

The worst thing about a night of alcoholic excess was that things came to you in fragmented pieces. My head was throbbing. I reached for the aspirin, then onward to the kitchen, to a clean-ish tumbler, filled it with ice-cold water, the plop of a pill, with a loud fizz to follow. My mind was so fuzzed I wanted to crawl back to bed, but already it was the afternoon. I heard Lisa in high spirits singing in the shower and the previous night's action slowly came into focus. Then the key in the bathroom lock turned, Lisa emerged smelling like a Provençal summer meadow, wild flowers and lavender. She appeared as though last night's excess hadn't happened. Her as yet unlined eyes shone and her skin glowed.

116

'Ouch Issy, you look like you had a rough night.'

I suddenly felt my age. 'Where did you disappear to?'

'That would be telling,' she teased.

'Ah, go on,' I ventured.

'Why, are you interested?'

'No . . .'

She was so tricksy. I followed her towards her room, hoping to spot an unkempt bed or even the ACTOR.

'Better grab the shower while it's free, Issy, I'm just getting dressed,' and she closed the door in my face.

Fiona was right, she was a total operator! There was Geraldine in hospital, probably dying, and she was already playing around. The problem for me was going to be getting the hard evidence, catching her *in flagrante*, as it were.

In the meantime though, we had tickets to sell.

So over the next couple of days I found myself stomping up and down the Royal Mile in the constant and unremitting drizzle, giving out leaflets advertising our show. This was the abominable process known as flyering, which I grew to loathe. Essentially you did battle with every other show at the Festival to try to coax people to come to see your show. Flyering was what Coke was to teeth: a spirit corroder. It was that hidden extra, the unread small print on the contract, which I, in my official rank, was expected to spend three to four hours of each day doing.

THE ART OF FLYERING (or how not to do it)

LOOK AT ME, I'M A PERFORMER.
 (Please come to my show, please come to my show.)
I'M BRILLIANT, LOOK AT ME.
 (It's a female comedy show. The Late Night Titter
Club.)
 I'M THE NEXT BIG THING.
 (It's quite funny. No, we don't get our tits out.)

(Me) standing beside the ACTOR on the Royal Mile
attempting to give out flyers as hordes of people filed
past us. One of us was doing better than the other.

I'VE BEEN ON TV!
 (Would you like a flyer? Oh . . .) turning toward the
ACTOR and addressing him (I knew I recognised you.)
 YOU ARE TALKING TO THE BLOKE SITTING
IN THE PIZZA HUT AD, LEFT OF SCREEN, NEAR
TOP.
 (Cool.)
 HAVE YOU EVER BEEN ON TV?
 (No.)
 DIDN'T THINK SO.
 Back to the punter. (Tonight we are doing two-for-
one tickets. Interested? It's for a good cause . . . mine
and the other performers'. Oh, okay, look I have a
couple of freebies – but don't tell anyone. You sure?
It's free. Honestly, it is a really funny show.)
 I'M A FUCKING GENIUS.

118

Me still trying to entice punter. (What? You want me to flash you my tits now? Right now? I'm a mother!) then to ACTOR (knew that would change his mind.)

RIGHTO, THAT'S ME DONE, I'M OFF. WE MAY WELL HAVE A FULL HOUSE TONIGHT. HOW YOU DOING LISSY?

(It's Issy . . . mmm . . . okay, I suppose. Oh CRISPIN, I meant to ask, how did it go the other night with Lisa?)

TOP GIRL! BEAUTIFUL CREATURE. THANKS FOR INTRODUCING US.

(And did you two . . . you know . . .)

DEFINITELY NOT A LESBO. SAME TIME, SAME PLACE TOMORROW, IZ?

(Sure, see you then.) Big inward breath and (Hi, I wonder if you'd be interested in an all-female comedy show?)

And so I continued, trying my damnedest to sell tickets and taking each rejection personally.

Thanks but no thanks.

And there were times when I felt quite desperate.

(Partial nudity guaranteed. Yes, guaranteed! The Mingers perform topless.)

Then, from out of the rolling mist Adrian emerged and in response to my, 'Damp, cold and freezing,' he put his arms around me, lifted me off the ground and shook me like a salt cellar.

'How many tickets you sold?'

'About ten.' Interest had risen dramatically with the 'topless comedienne' outright lie.

'Enough for a preview,' surmised Adrian. 'Come on, time for a break,' and he took me by the hand and introduced me to the most sinfully luscious Chocolate Soup Café.

CAUGHT OUT THERE

'So, this is what you get up to when you're meant to be flyering.' Lisa bounced up to us, looking very chirpy, her tone accusatory.

'Merely indulging in a moment of respite, though I've sold ten tickets, not bad for a preview, right?'

'That's bullshit,' she scoffed. 'Issy, this show is my future. Five years from now when I hit thirty the last thing I want to be is some loser, doing a crappy job and living on past dreams.'

'Lisa, believe me, neither do I.'

'You're already way over thirty.'

Jesus, but her tongue was sharp. Adrian made an effort to come to my defence. 'So how many tickets have you sold, Lisa?'

'One, but he's a casting agent.'

'And what, that counts as ten?'

'Precisely.'

I was thrown back out into the damp to spend another couple of hours with a goody bag full of two-for-one offers and freebie tickets, and even invested in a packet of Jaffa Cakes to sweet-talk prospective customers.

The turnout was an impressive twenty and the preview show went well enough, though Lisa's casting agent never appeared.

'YOU OK, ISSY? YOU SEEM A BIT DEFLATED'

The second preview night was over and all had gone satisfactorily enough. The audience this time had numbered fifteen. 'I'm fine, Adrian,' I fibbed. We had left the Caves and were on our way over to the Library Bar. I'd just received a very disconcerting call from Nadia regarding the Arthur Penn case. Further discoveries revealed Arthur Penn had fallen foul of a psychotic named Darren Deacon. A long-term psychiatric patient, Darren had been released into the community for sane behaviour seven years ago. Arthur Penn had employed him as his gardener and for three years all seemingly went well, or at least until Arthur discovered Darren was trying to steal his identity. Apparently Arthur had made complaints to the police, but was informed that until actual violence occurred, there was nothing they or he could do. Darren played on the edges of the law, took to stalking Arthur, taunting him from a safe distance and such like. Then his mental state got the better of him and he began dressing as Arthur, turning up at Arthur's place of work, at his club, at his doctor's and, finally, one night in Arthur's bed. Nadia didn't go into details, but it would seem that it was a fairly gruesome murder.

Darren was arrested and was to be put in Broadmoor Hospital, only on his way there the high-security van was involved in a pile-up and Darren managed to escape. Since then he'd been on the run.

'Issy, we're going to have to go to the police about this.'

My heart sank, shocked by the gravity of the situation. It was safe to surmise that the Arthur Penn I'd been following was the psychotic Darren playing Arthur.

'Jesus, Nadia, I'd been following him for months.'

'I know, Issy, I've already talked to Trisha and Fiona.'

'What do they think?'

'They're worried. We have a meeting with Bambuss tomorrow.'

I'd never really considered my job as dangerous. Flirting with other people's partners was hardly daredevil stuff. Worst-case scenario was a Black Betty, otherwise known as an emotionally skewered partner viciously lungeing at you. I'd experienced that once and come out the other end with a bruised ego and black eye, but that was it. In the main you got thwarted partners labelling you a prick-tease. The reality of having followed a psychotic murderer at his request and then him vanishing sat as uncomfortably in my mind as a fishbone would in my throat. A dangerous guy who knew me and most probably all about me was on the loose. This notion brought me back to Fiona's recent words when she mentioned she'd seen him near the office.

'You coming in, Issy?' Adrian asked, interrupting my pensive state, the pair of us having reached Bristo Square.

'Sure,' I replied, 'I'll be there in a while.'

I needed some time on my own, some space to ponder. My thoughts had turned to Max and suddenly I felt desperately vulnerable, emotionally adrift and overwhelmingly lost within a situation not of my own making, for once.

A (WO)MAN WALKED INTO A BAR . . .

There was once a woman who longed for a parrot or panda or monkey or some exotic animal to accompany her, and also for a bartender straight out of *Cheers*, with rapier wit, good looks and charm. Where, indeed, were all the people who knew her name? After three gin and tonics downed with some urgency, she decided they were trapped inside a small black rectangular box-like object under numerical codes. She checked the hour, but it was beyond calling time for ninety-nine per cent of contacts. Happy with that one per cent and by then on her fourth gin and tonic, she texted Scarface.

'Are you awake? I need to talk to you.'

Receiving no reply, and having consumed her fifth gin and tonic she called him.

'Scarface, I need to talk to you. Where are you?' She

started sobbing then, 'Scarface, you . . . Damn, why are you with her and not me? Why am I here and not there? Scarface . . . I'm sorry, okay? Sometimes I wish it could be different and that we could love each other, be in love with each other and then I realise, I don't really love you at all. I'm just projecting who I think I would love to be in love with on to you. Maybe if you were someone else I could love you. But you are you and you're a big shit, to be honest.'

Just at that moment her number-one choice brushed by her. He mouthed the words, 'You okay?'

She nodded, embarrassed to be caught at such a vulnerable moment, and he hesitated before continuing on his way.

DAMN, THAT WASN'T MEANT TO HAPPEN

Downing a sixth gin and tonic, I dried my eyes and called again. 'Hi, Scarface, it's me. Listen, ignore the previous message. I'm out of sorts, not feeling myself. This whole festival, this comedy thing, work stuff, it's much harder than anticipated. Guess I'm a little homesick and took it out on you. Cheers.'

Dear Max,
It's very, very early in the morning and I really should be tucked up in bed asleep, but instead I am thinking of you and how much I love you, which is close on

124

infinity times infinity, or about as much as anyone can quantify anything. Max, I miss your smell, smile, voice and all the silly jokes we share – like the time we were pretending to be opera singers and ended up performing a Gilbert and Sullivan light operetta in our kitchen. I was claiming you had my bum[1] and you, singing soprano, denied it.[2] Do you remember?

The apartment I am staying in is totally disgusting, my room is even worse than Harry Potter's room under the stairs. Imagine that. It doesn't even have a window. I call it the flea sanctuary or, since I cleaned it, flea cemetery. The only decent room in the place is the kitchen. It has a good view of the city. I can see two church steeples from the kitchen window and if I poke my head out, and stand at a strange angle, I can just about see Edinburgh Castle. It is super-wicked. Supersonic wicked. I'll take some photos and send them to you. Every day I have to try to sell tickets to the show. It's such a pain, all day trudging up and down the Royal Mile trying to be nice to everyone. We're done with the previews, the practice shows and tonight is the official opening show. All of us are on tenterhooks. Lisa, one of the other performers, has it on good faith that there will be lots of newspaper reporters there. Yikes, I am so nervous, Max, as nervous as you felt on your first day of school when I had to peel you off me. You were terrifically brave and I now know exactly how you felt . . .

*   *   *

1 'Your bum's the very model of my pre-motherhood posterior, and from where I'm looking it seems terribly familiar.'
2 No I don't, Yes you do, etc

'Issy, think about the performance; nothing else, the performance. Got it?'

'Adrian I'm freaking.'

'Focus, keep your focus.'

Honestly, how was I expected to keep my focus, considering Nadia's little update. Believing in the haunting presence of Arthur had been so much easier to swallow than the psychotic reality but, as they say in this business, the show must go on. I had to shake off all the extraneous stuff I was drenched in and concentrate on this opportunity, my future, my long-held dream. Adrian seemed to have taken a shine to me and put me under his wing. He was my acting protector, not to mention comedic coach. We'd been rehearsing my set for nigh on three hours, my nerves all a-jangle.

'Take a deep breath, concentrate on what you are saying . . . talk to the audience.'

'Yeah okay, talk, make like it's a conversation. What if I freeze, Adrian?'

'You won't.'

'Go blank?'

'You won't.'

'Forget the script?'

'That's the same as blanking.'

'Trip?'

'Get up.'

'Dry mouth?'

'Bring a glass of water.'

126

'An attack of flatulence?'

'Stand further back stage.'

'What if I'm running up on to the stage with my water and I trip. The glass smashes, sending splinters throughout the entire auditorium and suddenly I look up and the audience is covered in blood, and are so angry with me that I crap myself there and then and because of the costume they think I really am a nurse and . . .'

'Get a plastic glass.'

'Nice one, didn't think of that.'

'Enjoy it, Issy. You are in control.'

'What if they don't laugh?'

'They will. Your act is funny.'

FIRST NIGHT

I was running on fear, running late, splashing in piss puddles down dark Edinburgh closes, running my lines through different scenarios in my head, to the Caves, to the downstairs dressing room, to a standstill and there were the Mingers and Lisa. All of us in our pre-performance warped mental zone, otherwise known as Adrenalin Central, Anxiety Capital, State of Distress.

Then . . .

And I guess this was it for me, the opportunity I'd so longed for, the doorway to the future.

'Ladies and gentlemen . . .'

Some have rabbit's feet, others holy relics. Lisa had a double vodka and tonic and gushed over the huge bouquet of flowers she'd received from a mysterious admirer, while the Mingers chugged on fags. I had a quick prayer and Adrian had the audience in the palm of his hand. He was on stage warming up the punters. The house was fairly packed, my heart bouncing from my stomach to my throat. I was gearing up for my mad dash down the gangway.

'The one, the only.' The MC crossed himself.

Here goes everything, girl . . .

'A close, personal, showbiz friend of mine.'

Nothing was going stop me. The journalists would pick me out.

'All the way from north London.'

Well, you've got to start somewhere.

'Little . . .'

Hollywood, here I come.

'. . . Issy Brodsky . . .'

Go girl. Go girl.

Dressed in my ridiculous nurse's outfit, singing 'You Sexy Thing' by Hot Chocolate, I was off, running along the cobbled floor, jumped on to the stage, faced the back wall for a nano-second, twirled round to the audience, smiling. And there, sitting in the front row was the ACTOR and, beside him . . .

*   *   *

FOCUS, BRODSKY . . .

A performer must focus, empty the mind of all other thoughts, concentrate only on the words of the set. Surrender to the moment, be in the moment, it'll only take a moment and I promise it won't hurt too much.

Good evening, Edinboro, and how are you? Well?

A few encouraging murmurings from the audience.

Phew, 'cause I'm not really a nurse.

A ripple of a response.

No honestly. I bought it for my boyfriend. To help in the bedroom department (wink, wink). *He's a hypochondriac. Ah, no he isn't. Actually, he is. My boyfriend, Derek, he's always on at me* (shit, art does imitate life!!) *with his double entendres: I hate your fucking guts; his subtle innuendos: get out of my fucking life; and his total and absolute denial of my existence.*

A nice group 'Arghhhh.'

But that's men for you. You can't live with them, you just can't live with them. Give them an inch they'll claim it's nine. One in the hand is worth two in the bush (but I wouldn't recommended it. A little bit cramped!).

And I couldn't be 100 per cent certain.

I, I, I . . .

I began stumbling over my lines.

I know what you're thinking . . .

My Oirish accent faltering.

You're thinking I really am a nurse. I'm not. Though I am a very caring person.

There was something about his eyes.

I'm also a woman of a certain age.

The way they slanted. The shape of his lips.

Mmm . . . an . . . an age many men are very prejudiced against, they're forever . . .

Losing the rhythm . . .

. . . assuming I'm out to get them.

Losing focus . . .

And, well, I am. That is my precise agenda.

Losing the crowd . . .

But, see, it wasn't always like that.

My panic spread like a red-wine stain on a crisp,
white cotton tablecloth. A cloth that was, in fact, an
heirloom of a (hypothetically speaking) new boyfriend
whose parents I was meeting for the very first time.

Flooded by a deluge of thoughts, I struggled to keep
the set going. My concentration fractured. I felt the
audience inwardly groan, shared in their embarrassment, conscious of every punchline missing its target.
Held in a 'pre-car-crash' state, where you saw the
oncoming truck and realised the end was nigh, my life
flashed before my eyes. I was forced to acknowledge
all the shit bits, fuck-ups, humiliations, disappoint-
ments, disasters, tragedies and hurts, all in one go.

Jesus Christ, for a lone individual, I'd certainly
racked up a disproportionate amount of life's debris.
Then again, the good stuff was so ultraviolet brilliant
and bedazzling, I had to squint.

HEY! PSST, BIG G

Is there anyone home?
   Oi, you up there, what's that?
   You're not ready for me?
   You're having a laugh.

Let me in, God, damn you.

Do something man, Father of Man, holy moly. I need a miracle, like now.

Immediately.

A distraction.

A power cut.

Come on, G, don't let me down.

G?

G?

'I'm waiting

I'm . . .

You . . . you . . .

Judas!

How could you forsake me in my hour of need?

Answer me, God damn it. This I hadn't expected. I mean, after all I've been through, you throw this into the mix. You've really pushed things to the limit.

BACK IN REAL TIME

There was nowhere to flee, too many to fight. The only option left was to freeze.

I froze.

'Tell us a joke,' someone yelled from the back.

One woman looked down, maybe out of respect.

'Oh,' I said in my mock Oirish accent. 'Oh, I must check my pulse 'cause I seem to be dying.' Lisa's advice to me in a situation such as this was to acknowledge defeat. 'It'll dissipate the tension and you'll get them back on side.' A bit like honking at the oncoming articulated lorry?

Well, guess what? It didn't work. Even the titters of embarrassment dried up. In other words, I gave the audience a noose with which to hang myself. I reeled off as much of my set as I could, while trying to skip as much as I could. The blood rushed to my head. I could smell my own fear, thinking 'get me out of here'. The audience were in complete agreement. My fragile ego was like a pulverised garlic segment, crushed, and I hated myself for having even put myself up there in the first place. Words now had a whole new meaning. I could fully comprehend what it was to be 'gutted', 'shamed' and 'mortified'. To have defecated in front of them would, in a way, have been less revealing.

There was no applause at the end of the set. I ran out of the Caves and banged into two audience members who had snuck out mid-death and were talking to Lisa.

'Christ, that was awful, it was so awful,' I wailed in whispers, totally distraught.

'Yeah, that was woeful,' they concurred.

'I bombed, it was . . .'

'Tragic,' they kindly finished for me.

'You don't want to wait around to see the other acts?' Lisa asked them.

'Life's too short,' one pointed out.

'It can't have been that bad,' Lisa joked.

Neither of the women laughed.

*   *   *

133

'Issy, you complete twat.' There and then Lisa accused me of trying to sabotage the show. 'How could you? We are going to look like . . . like amateurs. You are so selfish.'

'I'm sorry. It wasn't intentional.'

'There are meant to be five reviewers in tonight. Guess we can wave goodbye to getting four stars.' Her total lack of empathy added nicely to the emotional state I found myself in.

'I'm sorry, Lisa.'

'What the fuck were you thinking?'

READER

I know what you're thinking. You're thinking it was Arthur Penn or Darren 'whatever his name was'. Go on admit it, that's exactly who you thought it was, but it wasn't psycho-face, you couldn't have been more wrong.

PARK LIFE

A few years back when Max was laying the foundations to a more conscious idea of his reality, I, falling in love with him time after time, was enraptured by his open curiosity and intense efforts to communicate. I believe children have an innate emotional intelligence, and noticed on park excursions how he would look at the fathers pushing their children on the swings. See, he was conscious even before the end of his first year that he did not have a father. The fear of every lone mother arose: that one's child will perceive every male as a potential daddy, run up to them, arms open and dribbling, with a two-syllable question begging to be answered, 'Dada?'

And then one day he asked, 'Max dada?'

'No dada.' I shook my head and said reassuringly, 'Max has Grandpa and Freddie.'

Aware of how important it was to provide Max with male role models, I'd had to rely on my father and brother. Luckily, they both, in their own way, met the challenge. My father had, by default, ended up spending a lot of time with us in the previous year and had an exceptionally strong bond with Max. Freddie was more the doting, spoiling uncle, buying Max's love with presents and trendy clothes. Although it was true that since he'd hooked up with his first proper boyfriend, he had begun taking Max out on mock happy-family outings, to musicals and films, I was very grateful for their strong presence in his young life and Max was happy enough. Then Scarface came along and Max was over the moon. He adored Scarface. He had asked me once if Scarface could be his dad, 'Please Mum, please, just for a while?' It was strange how his words rang true. As for Max's real father, well, see, it kind of, sort of . . .

OVER THE HILLS AND FAR, FAR AWAY . . .

Glastonbury in a field, in a tent, in love – okay, lust. It was a weekend of bliss, an accident of fate, and the rest as they say, is history. My Dutchman, Jan, disappeared into a sea of people, blowing kisses at me, and I thought, ah, this is the height of romance. It began as a random collision, removed from our respective realities and we unleashed ourselves on each other with an intensity I had never experienced before or after. In my mind it was more Austenesque than Erica Jongian. A perfect moment, so perfect I wanted only to capture it, to lock it away. I didn't want reality to intervene and redefine my hazy Super-8 impression into DVD clarity, besides which, at the time I was already in a steady relationship.

'What do you mean you'd forgotten when your last period was?' my mother asked. I was always crap with dates, and in my late twenties soon succumbed to the pull of biology. My role in life became clear – breeder – and my aforementioned relationship broke up.

There was something about the slant of his eyes and the shape of his lips . . .

*   *   *

IT COULD HAVE BEEN YOU!

A lottery, a swish of nylon and the dream comes true. In a single finger click, I spun round and immediately noticed the guy sitting to the left side of the ACTOR. Like a smack across the face, my heart strings went twang. It couldn't be, could it? How many faces had I scanned during the past five years and yet never had this feeling. All those escalators ridden and to no avail. The wishful thinking, the daddy daydreams:

1. I hear my name being called. 'Issy, Issy, is it really you?' I turn and see him. 'For so long I have searched. Oh, my darling!'
2. As above, but with the added element of Max. Jan gazing at Max, then back into my eyes, bursting into floods of tears and then sobbing, 'I dreamt of having a son, please tell me he is mine.' So I do. He swoops Max and I into his arms and twirls us round. In my mind he was always very strong.
3. As above, but quite out of breath and slightly elated I say, 'Jan, what are you doing in England? I thought you lived in Holland?' And he replies, 'I live here now. A great-aunt of mine has just left me her huge house in Notting Hill and ten million pounds cash.'
4. Continuing in the same vein, the three of us go to a café and over afternoon tea and cake fall in love, decide to get married and, arms linked, go home singing in harmony.

See, nothing too extravagant. All well within the realms of possibility. I like to think of myself as a very grounded person and not given to delusions. There was no alternative but to go back to the Caves to face him. My nerves were frayed, shaking from the emotional fallout. Yet in my heart I knew I had to go back. I had to, for my sake, for Max's sake, for God's sake, what if the man I saw sitting beside Crispin really, actually, beyond all reasonable doubt was Max's father? I mean sperm provider. Let's not blur the boundaries here. Good parenting has nothing to do with being able to breed, and vice versa. Morally though, did he have a right to know about the existence of his son?

'Excuse me, sir, just thought I should inform you that I used your sperm to create a living human being.' All it would take was for me to approach him and, surprise, surprise!

Blast from the past.

Well, well, who'd have thought it?

What you don't know won't hurt you.

No, that came out wrong.

How would I live with myself if I didn't at least ask/ tell?

God, why didn't I apply to that book club when I had the chance. I was always throwing away those unsolicited letters begging me to join 'at no extra cost' and avail myself of this month's fabulous offer on self-help manuals, such as *The Long-Lost Daddy Book:*

'an exhaustive guide on how to deal with finding the person you believe could possibly be the father of your child', or *Fleecing the Bastard the Legal Way* and its sequel, *Fleecing the Bastard Any Old Way*.

How do these book-club organisations get your details in the first place? This I'd ponder and then scrunch up the paper into a ball and think of all those millions and millions of trees sawn down for nothing. I mean, is there an established etiquette?

'Hi there stranger, long time no see.

'I got some news for you, buddy. Yep, you're looking at the bearer of good tidings.

'My name is Issy, does that ring any bells?

'Ting-a-ling-a-ling.

'Glastonbury?

'Tepee. Yours?

'Do you speak English?

'Well, I'm the mother of the son you never knew about.

'I tried to find you, but as we were only ever on first-name terms . . .

'I did put an ad in *Time Out*.

'Hey, Jan, don't run away.

'Hey, Jan, I swear, I'm not a crazy person.'

Seriously though, what would I say? What if he didn't remember me? What if he did? What if he had and that was why he'd come to the show and, having seen me die on my arse, would just pretend he didn't know me at all? What if he looked through me, beyond me, above me?

The agony of my death lingered and my future predicament filled me with intense dread. Mustering as much courage as I could, I snuck in again, hiding at the back by the lighting desk.

'Ladies and gentlemen, I think we can safely say, bar an initial hitch (the first act), this evening . . .' Adrian was rounding off the show and from the far corner Lisa gave me the thumbs-up and mouthed the words, 'Stormed it – I was brilliant.'

The Mingers sidled over to me. I could smell yesterday's alcohol off them. 'Jesus, Issy, that was one of the best deaths we've seen. It was so bad, it almost turned back on itself. It was almost funny.'

'Thanks,' I squeaked in reply, trying not to inhale too deeply.

'And congratulations, like.'

Oh, here we go. I braced myself for another bout of Brodsky bitchery.

'Thanks,' then graced them with my most sardonic smile.

'No girlie, we mean it. You're not a real comedian till you've died, so welcome to the club.'

Show over, the audience clapped and the lights came up. The venue had benches along the left and right sides and a gangway in the middle leading directly to the exits on either side. I stood at the back, close to the exit that wasn't going to be used and waited, half-hidden by the black curtain, hoping to catch sight of Jan.

*   *   *

TRAPPED

'Issy! Issy!' I could see Adrian waving to me from the other side of the gangway, beckoning me over. Positioning myself so close to the wrong exit suggested to the audience that it was the real exit, except of course it wasn't. There occurred a blockage, and much murmuring in the vein of, 'Oh, for God's sake.' Of course, having hoped to do my utmost not to draw attention to myself, inadvertently I had. So there I was in the throng of people, ushering them away from my vantage point and in the confusion, I tripped.

AND FELL STRAIGHT INTO THE ARMS OF JAN

'You okay?'
   'I slipped.'
   'What you doing?'
   'Looking for someone.'
   'Aren't we all.'
   I, the original lady from the Glasto swamp. With my waterproof poncho, bare feet and rolled-up combats, I literally fell into his arms in the quagmire that was the Festival that year. Carefree and open to anything that should cross my path and spark interest, he'd turned up.
   'I'm going to try and catch . . .' and before he could finish his sentence I added, 'Me too.'

He took my hand and we spent the next few days entwined. His tent 100 per cent waterproof (heaven), our mood calm, mellifluous and honey-dripping with desire. We were oblivious to all: every performer crooned for us, providing the perfect soundtrack to our show, we were the stars, we were the world, we were so off our faces it was 'beautiful', then one more kiss, just one more kiss, and there I was back amongst the common people.

SIX YEARS ON

'Tough call, Lizzy.' The ACTOR Crispin slapped me on the shoulder. 'Titanic, matey.' He pinched his nostrils closed and made like he was drowning. Lisa came up behind him.

'Don't be so cruel, Crispin.'

He lifted her up, swung her round, and said 'And as for you, my beauty . . .'

'Let me down,' she squealed flirtatiously.

He refused. 'Only if you promise to do what you did to me the other night.'

Oh, Christ. What had she done to him?

'Now, you brute,' she laughed. They were blocking the passage.

'Come on, Crispin, put her down,' I blurted, irate with the situation, and from the corner of my eye glimpsed Jan on the outward trundle.

I charged down the stairs, through the stone corridor and out on to the cobbled lane. At the corner a small crowd of audience members were slowly dispersing. A quick scan told me Jan wasn't amongst them. I looked left, looked right.[1] Damn, damn, he couldn't have got very far, if anywhere at all, probably he was at the Cave bar. Most people went there after the shows. I sprinted back inside. No mistake, it definitely was Jan, the eyes were the giveaway. Max has exquisite blue eyes. I'd forgotten how good-looking Jan was, pretty gorgeous actually. I don't mean to boast, but we're talking Jude Law territory. I know what you're thinking.

Me: Yeah, you, reader.
Undermining conscience/reader: So why would he be with you, then?
Me: Ever heard of the word personality?
Undermining conscience/reader: Yes.
Me: Well, if you're going to take that attitude.

Nah, you're right. See, pre-motherhood, I was a lot cuter and in much better shape, ie, I had one.

The Caves bar was rammed to capacity. Lisa caught hold of my elbow. 'The Casting Agent's here,' she whispered. 'He's buying me a drink.'

---

1 I could have crossed the road, there was no oncoming traffic.

'Great.'

'No need to sound so jealous, Issy.'

'Arghh, I wasn't, I'm looking for someone. That's great, Lisa.'

Betwixt, between each room I rushed. Searching among the crowd, I was a crow nesting atop the stairwell, glanced over my shoulder and there he was at the bottom, a disappearing white rabbit.

'Brodsky, your round. Come on, cough up.' The Mingers launched themselves upon me.

'In a minute.'

'We're thirsty now.'

I pushed past them, back down the stairs, and outside after him. He was at the corner. A black cab pulled over and in he stepped and away it drove.

'Jan! Hey, Jan,' I shouted.

Fuming?

Enraged?

Infuriated?

I believe I had a paranormal experience of such intensity that when one of the Mingers stuck her Minger face out the window and hollered, 'Brodsky, it's time to get wasted,' I dutifully complied.

FALLOUT

The next morning I woke with a rumbling in my belly. Didn't feel good at all, my eyes sleep-stuck, closed for

144

fear that if they opened, the room would spin at the speed of light. The horrific memory of my death loomed like the latent terror of having Social Services take your child away by some bizarre twist of fate, where something is misconstrued and false accusations fly, taking root in a cowpat of conspiracy theories (does every mother suffer from this?).

On the way to oblivion, I'd stood right in the centre of the bar feeling desperate when a random bloke came by and said, 'Saw your act tonight. Bit of advice . . .'

'Ha!' I shrugged my shoulders. Punters were always bursting with good advice. 'Go on then, stranger, do your worst.' By that stage I was ready for anything.

'Don't give up the day job.'

A witty riposte lay somewhere buried in the debris of my mind. Unfortunately I couldn't find it offhand, distracted by his foul, fishy breath and the fact that I had spotted a remnant of his dinner in his heavy beard.

'Thanks, fabulous suggestion.'

Weird thing was, I meant it.

THE DAY JOB

It was so damn obvious. After all, I was a detective. Okay, so maybe not the best, but surely not the worst? I could find Jan. I *would* find Jan. Jan and I would be reunited and it would feel so good.

'Hey, and I'm not known in this business as Double D Agent Brodsky for nothing.'

'What you mumbling, Issy?' Adrian had found me slumped on the doorstep of the Caves (doorsteps were an early childhood comfort zone). Kindly he dragged me to a standing position and tumbled me into a cab along with Lisa and the Casting Agent, Lisa having blown Crispin out in favour of someone with real power.

'Issy, Crispin's a boy, this guy could get me a part.'

'But what about Geraldine? She's dying for you!' I appealed to her more human side.

'The only one dying tonight was you, Issy.'

Oh yeah, it was all coming back. On the way home the cab dropped Lisa and the agent off at his hotel. I drunkenly beseeched Lisa not to go in with him. She misinterpreted me, replying to the effect that I was finally facing up to my true sexual orientation and the agent whispered that if I wanted to, he wouldn't mind me joining in either. They retracted their offer when I mentioned I felt sick and asked the cabby to stop and the cabby replied he already had.

Last night had been too much for one delicate Brodsky to handle. In times such as these, there was only ever one thing to do. Lie very still and pull the covers over my head.

*   *   *

It was no use, my bladder dictated motion, forcing me up. I rose, showered, gorged myself on melted cheese sandwiches, chocolate digestives and a half-litre of coffee, then went straight back to bed. It was from there that I put a call through to my life-saver.

'Mum?'

'Darling, we were all thinking about you last night. How did the show go? How are you?' My mother's voice was reassuring, calming, familiar.

'Mmm.' The edges of my lips quivered. I was on the precipice of an outpouring, the words sardines in my mouth, awaiting the tin opener. Words like: I died, Mother, I died. My very being seeped out of my pores. Heal me Mother, cast some of your new-world magic my way.

'Are you still there, Issy?'

My voice small and squeaky. 'Mum, it didn't go as expected.'

'These things never do, honey.'

'No, Mum, it was awful, surpassing every humiliation ever encountered. And I mean ever . . .'

ISSY BRODSKY'S TOP FIVE ALL-TIME CLASSICS

Coming in at Number Five.

Nursery, a mere three years old. Nearly new, but old

enough to remember. Standing in the corner with my back to the class. I had been banished to what was for me the far end of the universe for having scribbled all over Tanya Dawson's drawing, an act instigated by her spitting on my picture. Regrettably for me, Tanya had a shrill, high-pitched shriek that went off like a rich man's house alarm, alerting the teacher to her distress and my culpability. In retrospect, my punishment of excommunication seemed to underline the differences between us. Tanya was a natural-born group leader[1] and I wasn't, so I got in trouble and was forevermore consigned to the social slag heap. Okay, so the slag bit didn't kick in till secondary school, but from that moment on I was spurned by the 'bitch group' and ended up hanging out with the only boy in class, actually the only boy in school, and his name was little Colin Greaves. We all pitied Colin, even his best friend, ie me, and ribbed him incessantly. To be honest, it was low-level bullying of the later-life-destroying type. His mum, a teacher, had joined the school mid-term, fresh from the Outer Hebrides and had been unable to find a more suitable school for Colin.

Number Four.

Quite literally a first-class moment. First class in infants' school, five years old, the harvest assembly,

1 Über-bitch. Last I heard of her, she was working for the EU as an MEP – natch.

in front of all the parents, crucifying the hymn 'Morning has broken'. Otherwise known as the projectile-vomit episode. All over Tanya (hee hee).

Number Three.

Experimenting with hair. I was going through one of those teenage stages. Thought I'd get mine cut short and dye it. Orange. Bad, bad decision, made worse by then, in my frustration, opting for the shaved Sinéad O'Connor look. With her huge eyes and pixie face, she could get away with it. Alas, moon-face here . . . 'Nothing Compares 2 U' was the tune sung at me when I walked along the school corridor. Then just to add to the shame of it I was, until my hair grew to a reasonable length, continually mistaken for a boy.

Number Two.

The 'I love you too much' accumulative humiliation of the besotted teenager. The hanging on to shreds of hope that he'd look in my direction, answer the phone, slow dance at the disco with me (he said no). The worst part being he was the funky new headmaster. Oh yeah. I remember hanging around places in case I'd bump into him, like school. The feeling of never, ever being able to get over him, yet not even having had him.

Number One.

The 'Bohemian Rhapsody', one. School concert this

time, going through my creative Expressionist period.[1]
Let's just leave it at that, too hideous for words.

'Don't worry, I'm sure all comedians have off-nights.'
'But that's not all. Mother, there's more . . .'
'Issy, darling, there's another call coming in. Stay on
the line and I'll get rid of it.'

ON DIVERSION

I suppressed the compulsion to shout out, 'Mother, I
want to regress way back, to before childhood, tod-
dlerdom, baby id. I want to press rewind all the way to
fusion. Okay, maybe not – I still hate thought of my
mother and father doing it. Let's stop at the twinkle in
the eye, or the fifth vodka and tonic. Know what? If
sperm had personality, I'd have been the one swimming
along nice and easy, minding my own beeswax, when
whoosh, a huge tremor would have catapulted me into
the nether regions of creativity. And then, having taken
the wrong route and nearly dead on my fin from
exhaustion, I'd see this huge boulder slowly rolling
toward me. Dear Christ, I'd have moaned, I'll be
swamped, swallowed, I'll never get out of here alive . . .'
Except that would be the irony, that would be
exactly how I did get out of there.

*   *   *

1 Check out *The Honey Trap*, page 117.

The phone died: either that or my mother was deserting me in my time of ultimate need, although being averse to the technological age, she'd more than likely ballsed up. Thankfully I had only to suffer a moment of self-pitying paranoia before my mobile rang. I picked it up.

It was Fiona. She sounded concerned. She said not to worry, but the police wanted to interview me about Arthur/Darren. She said Bambuss would be touch and that I was to try to recall every detail, or as much as I could about him. She mentioned that Arthur/Darren was considered to be a highly dangerous individual and wanted in three countries on three separate charges of identity theft, murder and six charges of damage to city parks. She said the Fentons had rented out their house to him under the assumption he was a fellow academic and on a sabbatical. She mentioned he was last sighted in the Midlands in a motorway café doing *The Times* crossword sporting a couple of days' worth of facial hair growth. She added if there was anything I wasn't telling her or wanted to tell her or needed to tell her, to speak now before the police took over. Then she asked when exactly was the last time I had seen him?

I said I couldn't remember. I said my current state was not conducive to rational thought, factual accuracy and that in the given circumstances could she wait twenty-four hours. I had other things more pressing on my mind and I would get back to her.

She asked how the case was going with regards to Lisa. I duly reported that Lisa had gone home with a casting agent the night before and as far as I knew had stayed over and I then asked if she would put me through to Trisha. She sounded surprised. 'You want to talk to Trisha?'

This was an unusual request; Trisha and I didn't do banter.

'Yeah, is she there?' I needed clear advice, a straight answer from a no-nonsense person and circumstances dictated that that person was Trisha.

On a rainy random afternoon long since gone, I'd found myself in the office with Trisha. I was doing some cold calling, which amounted to phoning people to ascertain if they were a) married and if so b) happy.

'Look, Mrs Jackson, all I can say is that now, legally, you can take into account his projected earnings too. I know you say he'd be difficult to tempt, but believe me, we have some hot chicks working here. Okay . . . well, if you change your mind, you have our number.'

Trisha was standing at the window looking out on to Parkway, when out of the blue she asked, 'Issy, what happened when you found out you were pregnant?'

'Got scared and burst out crying.'

'Seriously though, what did your boyfriend say?'

'He was heartbroken. I think I really hurt him.'

'But he dumped you?'

'Yeah, 'cause it wasn't his kid I was carrying.'

I recounted the story from the best bit, the conception, to the sad bit, having to tell Finn (the guy I'd been going out with for ages) that not only had I been unfaithful, I was also up the pole. It didn't go down well.

'You were brave bringing a stranger's child into the world.'

'Well, I was three months gone.'

'And did you consider you know . . .' Trisha couldn't say it, the word 'abortion'.

'Too late.'

'I was always against . . . you know.' Trisha was an adoptee, for her it was a more loaded dilemma.

'It's a hard decision to make.'

'Would you have, or have you ever had to . . .'

'Luckily, no.' Many of my girlfriends had had to suffer that moral predicament. Some treated it as contraception, yet for others it was the hardest decision to have to take and many were filled with regret.

Trisha started crying. 'Issy, I never thought I'd be in this situation.'

That's life for you, hey. Always challenging, pushing you to the limits, catching you offguard and presenting you with worst-case scenarios. Oh, how the experience of life likes to make hypocrites of us all. Much akin to marriage and fidelity. How easily cherished ideals fall prey to the reality of long-term commitment.

'What if it, Issy, you know, it happened to you now?'

'Dunno.' I shrugged my shoulders. 'I guess it would depend on the circumstances of conception and where I was in my life. It's such a personal decision.'

Trisha was a divorcee with three teenage kids and not long to go before the nest was empty. She looked pained, her thoughts a mass of conflictions. She had only just hooked up with her much younger man. In one respect, motherhood killed the romantic in me. It's a big deal raising a child and, for most of us in the West, a conscious decision.

'Trish, unless I felt that primal urge to have another, honestly I don't think I would. Kids need a lot of nurturing.'

'Yep, you're right,' she said, recovering form and setting back to work.

'Issy, what do you want?' ever the non-emotional, cut to the core, no namby-pambying Trisha barked down the phone.

'Advice,' I replied.

'Spit it out.'

'I saw Max's father last night.'

'Did he recognise you?'

'Don't think so.'

'And . . .'

'Trisha, do you think I should try to find him?'

'Do you want to?'

'I don't know.'

Thing was, if I did find Jan, I'd would have to rework the messianic child story I'd so laboriously concocted. There was no way I'd be able to fob Maxy off with it any longer. To be honest he'd already outgrown it. Recently a local priest gave an assembly at his school and announced, 'We are all God's children,' much to Max's confusion. He grappled with the concept and asked if I could fix a play date with his brother Jesus 'cause he wanted to meet him. Tempted to offer up the standard 'lost hero/soldier' saga, sweetened with an Action Man, I'd held back, unconvinced. It was too easy, lazy lone parenting, if you ask me. Sure, I'd even toyed with the idea of claiming Max was born of angel seedling, though alien spawn would, for Max, be a more kudos-garnering option.

My head pounded with the mind-boggling complexities of human nature, blood being thicker and, though Max had strong 'father figures' in his life, they would most probably never negate the primal desire to search for and discover his actual biological roots. So I put myself in Max's position and tried to see it from his point of view (we're talking seriously low level, three-foot-something) and concluded that I would be undeniably peeved if my mother, having sighted my biological father, hadn't at least done her utmost to track him down.

Trisha urged caution, extreme caution. She had tried to seek out her natural parents, though the search proved disappointing. Her mother didn't want to

155

know and Trisha's subsequent appeal to her to reveal who her father was backfired when the mother hinted at abuse. Trisha had definitely not wanted to know that. In retrospect she said she'd rather have held on to the romantic belief that she was born of a Romeo and Juliet scenario.

Trisha suggested I do one of two things: try to befriend him to see if there was any common bond, or do nothing. 'Brodsky, my advice would be to go very slowly. No rash or hasty decisions. You know how men are, always the hunter, never the prey. Oh, and Brodsky . . .'

'Yes?' I asked guardedly, hoping she wasn't going to bring up the Arthur Penn case again.

'Good luck.'

THERE WAS IN EDINBURGH A WOMAN ON A MISSION, ON A MISSION (WELL, I RECKONED I'D HAVE KICKED MYSELF IF I DIDN'T AT LEAST TRY TO TRACK HIM DOWN)

Issy Brodsky, Double D super-agent found herself once more in the third person with a howling hangover and a decision taken. She decided to act with caution. Merely having found Jan unburdened her of a heaviness within and an emotional relief such that she consequently lost two pounds.

It dawned on her there was a high-percentage chance that Jan was involved in the Festival. However tangential, he was most probably a performer, actor, director, dancer, writer, artist or filmmaker. It made sense; most people in Edinburgh in August were linked to the arts, providing her with a starting point, a thread of logic to clutch on to, rather than to randomly scour the streets while out leafleting. So, over the next few days she would check through all Festival brochures, programmes and suchlike for Dutch or European productions. She would knock on every administrator's door requesting to see cast lists. With vigour she was determined to try every method known to man to find Jan or any permutation of his name: Yan, Yann, Janek, Johann, John.

IN THE MEANTIME, DEATH AND RESURRECTION TOOK PRIORITY

Lisa had summoned me to her bedroom, in which every daily paper – broadsheet, tabloid – was strewn across her bed.

'I've checked: nothing. Not one word has been written about us.'

I couldn't decipher whether she was disappointed or relieved.

'Issy, consider yourself incredibly lucky.'

There, I decided, was a novel way of interpreting my circumstances. See, none of the reviewers had turned up to our show, having been tempted away by the opening of another much more interesting show with far higher-profile actors and free booze. We Tits would have to get in line and patiently wait our turn. It was a double-edged sword. The whole review system could and did make or break a show, never mind the performers' egos. Get a stinker of a review and the show dies, unless, that is, you can edit out all the negatives – which absolutely everyone does. Get a good one, or even a fairly good one, and it's easier to coax an audience in off the street. The worst situation was to be ignored by the reviewers, as you would find yourself in review limbo, not professional enough even to warrant one. Never underestimate the audience; they are savvy, sophisticated and know the Edinburgh ropes – they are also the key to breaking even financially.

'I suppose you are really missing your son,' Lisa began kindly.

'Like a severed limb,' I replied. During one of our many phone conversations, my young son had said something that sent me askew.

'Mum, only eighteen more days to go.' He had been counting the days.

'Lisa it was like someone had a fistful of my intestines and was twisting them.'

'Exactly,' Lisa proclaimed. 'If it's too much for you, Issy, you could always, well . . .'

U2's 'With or Without You' was playing on the radio.

'What?'

'Issy, if you think you can't go on, continue with the show, I'll, *we'll* understand. I mean, I'll help you sort it with Geraldine.'

'God no!' I protested. 'Lisa, there is no way I'd let you all down, I promise, I swear to you. No way would I even consider leaving the show.'

Yep, in the face of death and emotional nuclear fallout from seeing Max's father, I was adamant that performing at the Festival and launching myself on the comedy world was one opportunity I wasn't going to let slip by.

'Issy, between ourselves, if it's just your pride keeping you going, I can always do a longer set.' Lisa gently put her hand on my shoulder.

'Lisa,' I said, 'I'm really touched.' Actually I was astonished and slightly rattled by her suggestion.

'Tense more like,' she babbled, continuing to rub the base of my neck. 'Want me to give you a massage?'

'Hmm, okay.'

'Look, between ourselves, you know I think you're great, it's just the Mingers were a bit weird about you messing up and they called Geraldine and Geraldine called me . . .'

'They called Geraldine, in hospital?' I was astonished.

'She's out now. Issy, I'm just warning you that you're treading a fine line.'

159

I couldn't believe the Mingers could be so two-faced. I began to protest, but Lisa's digging fingers were unravelling firmly knit knots, dating back to Girl Guide badges.

'But . . . but . . . oh yeah, just there.'

THE SAYING AND THE DOING

I was shitting it. Sure, the intention was to perform again, but going back up on stage was to me of Everest proportions. Oddly, the two-faced Mingers saved me, credit where credit was due. Post-death they took me under their flabby, tattooed upper arms and pushed me up on stage.

'It's like falling off a horse.'

Riding, I explained, was categorically not my thing.

'All right then, pretend you're careering down a steep hill, you fall off your bike. What's the first thing you do?' Minger One asked.

And before I could even mentally form a response, Minger Two answered, 'First thing you do is get back on.'

'Not,' I contested, 'if the wheels are all mangled and my body is broken.'

Get a grip, woman, fight the darkness, spurn Satan, this ain't no suicide mission. Lady, are you a pussy-whipped bespectacled small man with a lisp and short on facial hair or just a big girl's blouse?

Yesirree, G. I gave voice to my evangelising funda-
mentalist within and faced the fear.

FACING THE FEAR

'I feel sick. I can't go on.'
  'Yes, you can.'
  'Can't.'
  'Ow!'
Okay so the Mingers' electrified cattle prod was
probably going slightly over the top, but it worked.
Over the next few days and nights I kept one eye on Lisa,
the other out for Jan, should he cross my path again, and
performance-wise grinned and bore it like a trooper.
Adrian offered me further sympathy and Lisa took me
out make-up shopping after enlightening me about the
fact that I suffered dreadfully from a shiny face and that
a bit of powder could make all the difference.

'IT COULD MAKE ALL THE DIFFERENCE . . .
ATTENTION TO DETAIL'

'Yes, yes, I realise.' I felt like I did at my doctors' when
she gave me advice about contraception. Like a thirty-
recurring woman wouldn't already know all there was
to know.

'Are you practising safe sex, Ms Brodsky?' my doctor would ask in her mock-concerned voice. I'd look at her blankly and in all seriousness reply, 'No, Doctor, I purposely go out of my way to pick up diseases so I can wait for hours on the phone to try to get an appointment and then spend more hours in the waiting room so I can have some stranger stick some God-awful instrument into me. It's a favourite pastime of mine.'

If there was one thing I hated, it was being treated like an idiot.

I could hear Bambuss chewing on a toothpick at the end of the line.

'I thought you and Maria were going on a cruise.'

'We were,' he snapped, the response loaded, weighted down by the implication that somehow I was to blame for it. 'Yes, Brodsky, my first holiday in fifteen years cut short. It was the *first* time since my wife's death I have taken off. Maria and I had been looking forward to it for a long while. We booked it last year. And then . . .'

'Bambuss, it's not my fault this lunatic is on the loose. Anyhow, why are *you* on this case? There's loads of really great detectives out there.'

'Wouldn't you know it, Brodsky, but I headed the original Arthur Penn murder investigation. Darren is my nemesis. I've been trying to track him down for years.'

'Oh well, in that case maybe you should change

tack. Your methods don't appear to have worked.' I loved winding Bambuss up.

'I wouldn't sound so smug if I was in your situation, Brodsky,' came his retort. He, too, enjoyed trying to freak me out.

'Why would that be, Bambuss?'

'Has it occurred to you that you could be Darren's next victim?'

'Of course, but you know me, I always maintain a positive attitude to life.' I'd held such a notion at bay, considering it more of an abstract concept, sure there was too much on my plate already. I knew what Bambuss was after. He wanted to creep me out, instil me with fear, try to coax me into some sting and use me as Darrenbait.

'Brodsky, there's no need for you to worry but . . .' Interestingly, both Nadia and Fiona had said the exact same thing to me. I had an inkling that when repeatedly told not to worry it is precisely what one should do. 'But for your own safety keep an extra-vigilant eye out at all times. Try not to be on your own.'

'Okey pokey, Bambuss.'

'It's no joke, Issy,' he said. 'This guy is dangerous, you could be next in line. I need to know everything, starting with the last time you saw him.'

'Well Bambuss, now here's the thing . . .'

The seriousness of my predicament dawned and I was forced to grass myself up, basically guaranteeing my own dismissal if the Trap got wind of it. In light of my cooperation I made Bambuss swear he would do his utmost not to say anything. Although ever since the finger incident (yes, you guessed it, you'll have to read that classic book *The Honey Trap* to find out), his seduction of Maria and the 'Soho fiasco', there existed an uneasy edge to our relationship. In common speak, considering all the grief I'd caused him, I wasn't sure how trustworthy his word was.

'Finding Darren is my life's ambition. If I do, I'll be knighted. If I am, then you and I, my dear Brodsky, are quits. But I need to know everything, all the details. Has he been in touch with you?'

'No.'

'You're positive?'

'Yes.'

'Think hard, any strange texts, cards, calls, encounters?' Bambuss probed. 'Anything you think could help us, Issy, call me, okay?'

I strained my brain, sieved my thoughts went through the past few months like an archaeologist. Nothing came to mind.

'AND HOW IS MY STAR?'

Uncertain whether Geraldine was being facetious, I replied, 'Thankfully my performances have begun to improve.'

'Not you, I'm talking about my Lisa,' she rasped before commencing a five-minute coughing fit. Geraldine was in recovery and out of hospital. We had all been instructed via Lisa to call and report in on our Festival experience. I felt for Geraldine, could scarcely imagine the trauma she must have been going through all alone in London while her true love was up in Edinburgh having, well, more than a good time.

'Lisa? Oh yeah, Lisa is good.'

'And you girls are having fun?'

'Loads,' I replied.

'Well, don't have too much. She told me you were a bit of a wild thing, Issy.'

Me wild? If only Geraldine knew what her love was getting up to or, in Lisa's case, down to.

'ON MY KNEES GIVING HIM THE BEST . . .'

I didn't want to know. I really didn't want to know. At least not the graphic details, the ins and outs, the . . . 'When I noticed this green light.'

Lisa had summoned me to her room. She lay stretched out on her bed surrounded by bouquets of flowers successfully camouflaging the hideous décor. She looked like a pretty girl in an advert, writhing on the bed in crisp clean white pants advertising those plug-in odour busters. You know the type, the ones that last for sixty days. I'd be cast as the frolicking, Labrador source of the pong. 'Isabel my head hurts, will you make me a cup of tea . . . and some toast?'

I was her 'Isabel' and a favour was traded for information. Hey, everyone has a price. So I tended to her requirements then lay like the loyal pup at the end of her bed listening to her munch, slurp and recount her most recent evening of debauchery with the Casting Agent; the experience inclusive of a Paris Hilton moment. Yep, talk about overexposure. I mean, imagine the mortification of big bunny-eyed Hilton, to be so cruelly and doubly shafted? It's a wonder the young heiress didn't go off the rails. On the contrary, Paris made the experience work for her, even got a TV deal off the back of it.[1]

'All the guy had to do was ask. I mean, I'm an actress. I do like being filmed. It's basic good manners, is it not, Isabel, to ask?'

'What about Geraldine? Don't you feel guilty?'

'No,' came the abrupt reply. 'You're jealous, admit it. It's written all over your face.'

'Me, jealous? As if,' I snorted.

'Then why so curious?'

'But, what if Geraldine finds out?'

'How will she find out?'

'Adrian saw you.'

'Don't worry about Adrian, he's cool. The Casting Agent would be an idiot to say anything, so that leaves just you.' She gave me one of those deep, penetrating stares of hers. Made me feel nervy, naked, thirsty.

1 Note to self: when famous must get Paris's shrink's number.

'You can trust me. Promise.' My fingers criss-crossed my chest.

'But that's it, Issy, there's something about you. I think you're holding back on me.' She dangled her newly painted fingers in my face.

'Don't be silly,' I implored, 'I feel really close to you Lisa, I consider you a good friend.' I'd latched on to Lisa pretty firmly and, if I did say so myself, played the sycophantic ugly best mate with aplomb. She loved it and, to be honest, it worked for me too. Edinburgh was an intimidating place, a place where everyone seemed to know everyone else, though not me. In a way, it was like being at a party every night, only to discover that it wasn't 'the' party. Cool things only ever happened at 'the' party. Lisa may have been my mission suspect but she was also one of the few people I knew in Edinburgh well enough to hang out with and who had access to some of 'the' parties. 'Lisa, don't get me wrong, I'm not judging you but, it's . . . I dunno, I find it strange that you seem to be ignoring how ill Geraldine is. Cancer is deadly serious.'

She nearly gagged. 'Shit, Issy, cancer? So . . . so that's why you're always asking me about Geraldine! You think I'm a total bitch.'

'Well, yeah.'

She was laughing, shaking her head in disbelief. 'You twit. Geraldine is much more than a fuck to me, she's . . . she's . . .' (A meal-ticket? A career move? A deep physiological response to her relationship with her mother?)

167

I interrupted Lisa with, 'Is your mum still alive?'

'My mum? What's she got to do with Geraldine? The thing is, society wastes too much time equating being emotionally faithful to someone with sexual fidelity, don't you think, Isabel?'

'Who knows, different strokes for . . .'

I enjoyed our girlie moments – it felt slightly reminiscent of boarding school, or what it would have been like to have gone to one. Secretly, I'd always wanted to go, but my mother abhorred the English tiered education system and sent me to a comprehensive for political reasons.

Massaging Lisa's feet, I listened as she passionately argued her case. Being an amoral bisexual, she'd probably make a great agent provocateur, I surmised, so it was a pity Fiona loathed her so much. Lisa purred at my massaging efforts. She was being over-gracious, lying back on the bed. The meditative rhythm was calming, head-clearing for me. All of my experiences of late could, I figured, be piled up, salvaged and put to good use. On the plus side I was amassing mounds of material and the mere thought filled me with a surge of positivism, triggering the realisation that I'd enough for an hour-long solo stand-up show.

'Magical hands,' sighed Lisa. 'You got the touch, Brodsky.'

'You said it,' I agreed. 'So, Lisa, are you seeing that Casting Agent again?'

'Don't know. The guy's a plonker,' she sighed. 'Yesterday he said he wanted me to audition for a part in a sitcom.' She announced this like it was the end of the world.

'That's so cool,' I shrieked.

'What? A measly audition, I was like, dickhead? Audition? Are you for real?'

'What did he say?' You had to admire her chutzpah and okay, it had to be said, flawless body.

'He assured me it was purely protocol, swore the part was definitely mine. He wants me to read against the auditionees. Isabel darl . . . would you do me a massive favour and do it?'

'How come you don't want to?'

'Get with the programme, it's like being an extra in a movie. Though for you it would definitely be a good experience.'

LOWEST OF THE LOW

Hierarchies everywhere. Everywhere. There I was, strictly bottom-rung. The show was a comedy pilot script for BBC3 entitled *The Parlour* and set in the reception room of a brothel. The characters were all puppets with Pinocchio complexes, wanting to be real girls and in one case, a boy. It reminded me in essence of the Honey Trap, though a lot sleazier.

In the lobby of the swish Caledonian Hotel, I spotted the Casting Agent. Caught him mid-bollocking, being chewed up and spat out by London's top comedy agent, Nell Tony. She was giving him a right mouthful.

'Nell, it's all under control. These are just preliminary auditions.' The guy was visibly quaking and she, unimpressed with his gravity-defying shape-shifting, turned to storm off and banged straight into yours truly. When I say banged, she tripped over me, landed on her posterior.

'Oh my God, I'm so sorry. Are you okay?'

'Fine,' she barked as I fussed and flustered about her, then took advantage of the situation.

'I'm a stand-up, Issy Brodsky. I'm . . .'

'I know. I remember you from the competition. You play the bunny boiler.'

'Irish nurse,' I corrected her.

'The bungling idiot.'

'That's me,' I laughed. 'Well not really me, the real me, look here,' and before I could do any further damage I handed her a flyer. 'Come to the show. I can get you comps,' I pleaded, which was like giving Harvey Weinstein two free tickets to the cinema.

'Fuck, fuck, fuck.' The Casting Agent spoke 'expletive' from the moment Nell was out of earshot all the way to the hotel room. 'She has me by the nuts.' From all accounts, she wasn't the only one.

'Who are you?' he asked, clearly unable to recall me from the cab incident.

'Lisa sent me.'

'Lisa sent you?'

'She said sorry she couldn't make it and hoped

you'd take me in her place.' I gave him a cutesy look, albeit one that had outlived its potency by about fifteen years. He shuddered.

'Hey mister, *not* in that way, but to read in at today's auditions.'

'Right,' then under his breath I heard him mutter, 'Fucking Lisa, bitch nearly cost me my job.'

'WHAT THE HELL ARE YOU DOING IN THERE?'

The Casting Agent peered at me menacingly.

'Just getting a video tape. You did ask me to get a tape didn't you?' Oopsa daisy, I must have veered off course into his bedroom and was innocently burrowing through his tapes marked personal. 'Sorry,' I apologised.

'Right, so we're all set. Ready to roll.'

I spent the entire afternoon reading against every sodding actress/comedienne at the Edinburgh Festival. In they traipsed, baring their souls to the video camera on the slim promise of stardom. Some would giggle, flash rave reviews, one brought in doughnuts as a treat (I liked her). There were nerves, neuroses, egos, no-showers, no-hopers and no way José's – even the Mingers came. Then last, but by no means least, Lisa arrived, fizzing confidence and giving it her all. She twirled her fingers through Shirley Temple ringlets, faced the cam-

171

era, winked and, flashing her dazzling smile, cooed, 'Whenever you're ready, Mr Casting Agent.'

And . . .

ACTION
EXT: RANDOM OFF-LICENCE, DAY

Issy Brodsky takes refuge beneath the awning of an off-licence when the measly, though consistent, drizzle turns into a heavy, battering downpour, a metaphor for her state of aching loneliness. In an unknown place, with unknown people, without any support, she treads unknown waters.

We chase the metaphor to its natural conclusion as our heroine experiences an example of Scottish dour humour. The manager of the off-licence, smiling and waving at her from inside, presses his finger on the switch to activate the automatic awning upwards. A sheet of water cascades down upon her. Skin drenched, she tries to hail a cab.

ISSY: Taxi!

As she hollers, a taxi draws up, only to splash her.

(Working title: *Issy Brodsky Versus Life*).

*   *   *

TAKE TWO
INT: FLEA-PIT FLAT LATE AFTERNOON

The fleapit apartment reflects the downbeat mood of our heroine and her helplessness in the circumstances she finds herself in. Issy Brodsky sits comfort-eating in the kitchen on the phone to her boss.

ISSY: Fiona, I have the evidence required.
FIONA: Good work, Brodsky, knew you'd deliver in the end.
ISSY: Well, they don't call me Double D Brodsky for nothing.
FIONA: They sure don't. Hope you're ready for our arrival.
ISSY: What do you mean?
FIONA: Our descent *en masse*.
ISSY: *In inglese per favore*.
FIONA: Nadia's hen party!

Damn, I knew there was something I'd forgotten. Fiona had come to the rescue magnificently. When Nadia revealed her pregnancy, having secured full maternity benefits, she also let slip that she'd put me in charge of the hen party. Fiona assured her it was under control and the Honey Trap were taking a jaunt up north to celebrate.

'Can't tell you how much we are all looking forward to hanging out with you showbiz types, experience some of that razzmatazz, indulge in some debauchery, soak up the glamour of the rich and famous.'

'Yeah, right,' I yelped, hoping they wouldn't be too disappointed with the reality.

REALITY

The Titter Club had hit a midway Festival lull with still no reviews, which made for dwindling audience numbers. It was getting progressively harder to pull punters in off the street. Lisa's performances were slipping and she blamed it on us. She suggested in the chummy tones of a Famous Five member that we all pull together and redouble our efforts on the flyering front, an observation that wouldn't have been so explosive if she had ever done any. Of late, the Mingers had been teasing Lisa, claiming she was a born-again Madonna-ist or a fundamental diva.

'At least I'm not a couple of fat slags,' she sneered and then abruptly ceased all communications with them.

Yep, there had commenced a battle of the egos at Lemming Terrace. Tensions were running high in the house, with patience in short supply. Someone kept forgetting to put the top back on the toothpaste (me), food had been plundered (not me), and all the mugs and cups had mysteriously disappeared (not me). Usual household niggles stacking up, piling high ready to collapse, and all made worse by the fact that we worked together. The Mingers were categorically not impressed. Added to this, they exposed Lisa as the mug thief. Seven were found in her room, lining the window pane. She was also deemed a biscuit thief (aka the food plunderer), exposed by the crumbs all over her sheets and, finally, a mere thief. Two of my CDs, their hairdryer and Epilady, and Adrian's iPod were all found in her wardrobe. The Mingers accused her of being a lying, thieving, scuzzy bitch and, in her defence, Lisa claimed she had just borrowed them.

A huge argument ensued. Minger One had to restrain Minger Two from giving Lisa a 'good slapping'. Lisa provoked the pair further with her superior education, mocking their baseness and predictive class behaviour. Adrian ended up restraining both Mingers and I offered to put on the kettle and make some tea.

We were entering week three of the Festival and our spirits were on the wane. To compound this, I had sat through two hours of student Strindberg, three 'dance performances', German stand-up, Belgian rockers, Dutch mime artists, short plays, shorter films, works in progress, cabaret, *komedie*. I had watched loads of young kids thinking they were presenting the world with a brand new, revolutionary, unique way of looking at things, which I'd seen done a million times before. I trawled the late-night bars with an added purpose besides inebriation, but nothing, nowt, *nada*, *rien*, zilch rendered since first I did glimpse Jan from the porch of death's door.

Ah, how disillusionment coloured my dreams of whirlwind success. The night before we'd had to cancel the show, as no one turned up and then came the evening of performing to just six people. One more than in the cast. We gave our audience a choice, their money back or us. Surprisingly, they chose the latter, forcing me to rethink the delivery of my act. Nurse Issy Brodsky was nothing if not over the top – halfway through I'd break into one of Meat Loaf's classic love ballads and serenade an unsuspecting member of the audiece with my off-key vocal tones and air guitar. I hazarded a guess that the only way it would work was to drastically adjust the volume and to whisper my set.

Oh, so quietly . . .

Ironically it proved to be our best show to date. What the audience lacked in quantity they made up for in generosity, being liberal with praise and salutary aftershow drinks.

Indeed, the evening of my whispered performance marked a turning point for me. Comedically I moved out of intensive care, the ward, the hospital and was in the taxi on the way home. From that evening onward, performance-wise I was on an upward trajectory, a little acorn ego was firmly taking root. I acquired an 'attitude' and it grew on me like an extra layer of skin. See, as a performer you need some amount of talent but, curiously, not that much. If you wanted to succeed as a comedian or even just succeed, you need rhino skin, a presidential determination and a fundamental-ist belief in yourself. I was learning a lot from Lisa and told her as much. She seemed genuinely touched. Sometimes there really was no room for self-doubt.

'COME ON ISABEL, YOU CAN DO IT'

Sunday afternoon. Lisa and I set out to conquer Arthur's Seat. I'd wanted to go to the Summer Fair with the Mingers, but had been put in an 'it's me or them' situation and was now being dragged jogging up the mountain. Too much alcohol and not enough exercise dictated physical punishment for me, while Lisa seemed to be taking it in her stride.

Running ahead of me, her blonde curls bobbed carefree in the rare, precious Scottish sunshine, her flat, fake-tanned midriff contrasting splendidly with her Juicy Couture tracksuit.

For the first time in weeks the wet weather was holding off and crowds appeared, along with the Fair that had set up on the Meadows. The fun was all-inclusive, and out crept the underclass, their pasty skin instantly breaking out in rashes on impact with fresh air. There was Mummy and Daddy Fuck-Up with their two wee ones out for the day. The youngest was the same age as Max and there all similarities ceased. His eyes were old, his face prematurely aged, his manners adult and shoulders hunched. He scurried forward, doing his best to keep up. The family stopped and sat themselves on a low wall, presenting a tight, united front and the father began playing with his son. He raised his hand as if to strike the boy, then at the last minute retracted it. The parents found this hilarious, the child relaxed a little and enjoyed the attention he was getting. He started to laugh and then the father whacked him for real.

WHAT YOU LOOKING AT?

The whole of Edinburgh lay before me. I'd made it to the top of Arthur's lap, and peered out across the landscape. I felt invincible, even though the steep ascent had given me a cardiac workout and, from my panting, one I was obviously in much need of. Gaining perspective, chest heaving, hands on what once was a waist, I collapsed at Lisa's feet, lay back in the long grass and let the weakest of rays shine directly on to me. Lisa sat beside me with her arms clasped round her knees.

'I spoke to Geraldine today,' she announced.

'How is she?'

'She sounded a little distant.'

'That's dying for you, the body slowly begins to shut down and you start disconnecting with the outside world. I'm sure she's really missing you.'

'Isabel, you're crazy! She's coming up this week.'

'Really?' I spluttered, surprised at her speedy recovery. Medicine just keeps getting better.[1] 'You looking forward to seeing her?'

'Mmm.' I resented Lisa's capacity to be so non-committal. Having initially labelled her an easy read, I found she was far more complex than envisioned. Over the past few nights she had calmed down on the predatory-female front and forgone any extra-curricular relationship activities. 'I saw your number-one choice, Jake Vincent, last night.' So wrapped up in my troubles I'd forgotten about my number-one choice. 'Apparently, he's a total womaniser.'

'How do you know?' I queried, eyebrows raised.

'I don't for sure, just what I've heard. I'm meant to be seeing him tonight,' she smiled coyly.

'Jesus, Lisa,' I exclaimed, totally miffed with that information, 'I am so jealous; first it was Crispin, then the Casting Agent, now Jake!'

She stretched out, turning on her side to face towards me. 'Hark at Miss Virtuous. Exactly how many guys have you had since the beginning of the Festival?'

'A big fat zero.'

Lisa gasped. 'Really?'

Loathed to admit it, but there you go.

*   *   *

1 I'm sure that phrase could be valuable to someone in the Department of Heath – they could use it in a public-service ad campaign.

179

Well, I'll be damned. A rare thing indeed in days like these. In animal terms I was a dodo. Shagging around was part of the contract. It was more than obligatory. It was compulsory. Performers were responsible for all show losses accrued, producers' fees, printing costs, etc, etc, and also for the casual spread of STDs. Remaining a Festival virgin was like a fat kid sitting in a candy store refusing to indulge.

'Not possible, Issy, unless of course you are . . .' What occurred next took me unawares. I was ambushed, straddled, Lisa's face looming over mine, her arms pinning mine down. 'I bet you're an undercover . . .'

'What?' Shit. 'What?' Don't say it. My first thought was she knew, had probably known for ages that I'd been tailing her, and the game was up.

'An undercover Sapphic.'

'Phew, what a relief,' I splurged, 'I mean . . .'

And then the sun eclipsed the moon and she, well, she kissed me.

Her lips on mine, the softness, the velvety softness.

Her tongue slowly easing my lips open, flickety flick . . .

Aye karumba . . . then straying into my mouth . . .

Holy moly . . . flirting with my tongue . . .

I tell you it was . . . it was . . .

It wasn't on.

Internal alarm bells rang out, Oh yea, oh yea, oh shit, my sexuality was in crisis, exchanging fluids with another woman, was I that desperate? This was all Scarface's fault. Could I be? Could I possibly be?

'Get off,' I yelled, coming up for air.

'Why, afraid you're enjoying it?'

'No.'

'Really?' She leaned over and kissed me again, inducing an all-over body tingle. Cruelly she laughed at my obvious arousal, flushed cheeks and pointy nipples.

'Yes, okay.' Christ, what was I doing? 'No,' I spluttered.

'You're so indecisive Issy, you should stop thinking, let go and . . .'

'Sorry Lisa, I can't do this.'

'Why? It's so apparent you fancy me.'

'I what? Really? Me fancy you? Look, I do think you're beautiful and you have a super body and you're clever . . .'

'See, I told you.'

'What I mean is, I'm flattered, but I can't kiss you.'

'Prick-tease.' She leapt up like a young bunny. She was messing with my head, she was definitely messing with my head. 'You coming?'

WHAT DO YOU MEAN 'YOU'RE COMING'?

My mother had just informed me of her and my father's intentions to come to Edinburgh for the last week.

'What about Max?'

181

'Oh, he's coming too.'

'But, but . . .'

'Don't worry, we aren't going to drop you in it, but it would be lovely if your father and I could have a weekend away together. Actually, sweetie, I have important news for you.'

'Don't tell me something is wrong with Max?'

'No, he's a total joy. It's your father. He's fallen in love.'

'Oh for God's sake, not again.'

'Yes. I . . .'

'Don't tell me, she's younger than him.'

'Yes, and she has kids.'

'A single mother! Hey, Mum, there's hope for us all.'

'And, well, we can't wait to see you, Issy. Max is being very brave but he misses you a lot.'

'Thanks a bunch!'

'It's fine, darling.'

'I mean for heaping on the guilt.' Ah, but parents do know just how to rile you, how to press those buttons. Lisa had caught the tail-end of our conversation and was winding me up, lolling about the kitchen in a pair of high heels and lace pants while – and this was the part that got me – eating a banana.

'Can you not do that?' I requested politely.

'Do what? Eat a banana?'

Yours truly was playing mum, cooking up a frittata and doing my utmost to ignore Lisa's blatant provocation.

'It's the way you're doing it,' I further observed.

She was undeniably doing it on purpose. Ever since our little incident she'd been teasing me, dangling herself in front of me. I mean if I'd had a wick, she would, as it were, have been getting on it.

'Chill, Issy, it's not like you've never seen a pair of tits before. Wanna feel?'

'No thanks, I'll give it a miss this time.'

'Certain?' Both hands cupped her breasts, she was offering them to me, practically rubbing herself up against me and that's when Minger One burst into the kitchen.

'I WASN'T FONDLING HER NIPPLES!'

'Course not,' Minger One winked.

Lisa had excused herself, then slunk off into town to get her roots done, leaving me all alone with the Minger.

'Lovely omelette Issy, ta,' she said punctuating the end of the sentence with a very loud and resonating belch.

'It was a frittata.'

'So where did Her Royal Highness say she was going?'

I pointed to my head.

'Personality transplant?' Minger One smiled. 'We can but hope.' Her smile stuck as she picked a piece of courgette out from her teeth.

'She's not that bad,' I argued.

'I forgot. You and Lisa have a "special relationship". You do know Geraldine's on her way up.'

'What?'

'Geraldine is coming.'

'I didn't mean that. It was the bit about us having a special relationship.'

She put two fingers up to her mouth and made a crude gesture from which one could only draw but one conclusion. And then it came to light that the Mingers, Adrian and all the Cave staff were under the impression Lisa and I were having a ding-diddly, you know what, a wadjamicallit, toot-toot. Stunned, I near choked on my tea and spent the next five minutes having a coughing fit.

'Issy, no point denying it. Look it, you've been hanging out with her for weeks. Everyone calls you her shadow, you're like a besotted teen.'

Spluttering, gasping, I did my best to set the record straight, categorically denying my involvement. I vehemently protested my innocence, to the point of sounding like an old record, 'No nay never no more.'

'Yeah – but like, if you're not doing her, who are you doing?'

'No one!'

'Expect me to believe that? Get real, Issy, I wasn't born in the last century.'

Ever felt like hitting your head off the wall repeatedly?

Well don't.

It hurts.

'Ow,' I appealed to the Minger beseechingly, 'honestly, there is nothing going on between us.'

'I don't give a shit. But I'm warning you, if Geraldine

finds out, she'll go ballistic. She's got quite a jealous streak in her.'

'Read my lips, Minger, Lisa and I . . .'

'. . . Were seen kissing up at Arthur's Seat.'

CHRIST, WHY ME?

Stumped for an answer, I slumped, defeated, down in a chair

'And if you want my opinion, you're too good for her,' Minger One continued.

Oh, what was the point any more.

'Thanks, that's nice to know.'

The bathroom door swung open and a waft of cheap aftershave hit me full on.

'Aye, aye, beautiful.' Adrian stood blocking the doorway, then added, 'Not you Issy.'

I looked at him in disbelief. If it wasn't me, that left only one other person and that person was a Minger. Taking a glance to my left I found that person blushing. Adrian winked at her, then plodded on. Astonished, I demanded the details, whys and wherefores.

'We heard he was extraordinarily well endowed.'

'We!'

'We're twins, we share everything.'

'And?' I asked.

Up she stood and staggered over to the kettle.

*   *   *

Lisa said she couldn't care less about what the Mingers thought or who they did. As long as I kept a comfortable distance, Geraldine wouldn't cotton on. 'She's a complete muffin,' Lisa declared.

The Muffin's arrival was imminent, with the Honeys in hot pursuit. I'd had a quick debriefing with Fiona with regards to Lisa. 'Any more conquests?' she'd enquired.

I refuted any knowledge of wrongdoings. Christ, the thought of the office hearing about my latest Lisa antics would have been like a repeat of the Dirty Bob fiasco and the last thing I needed.

'Good to hear. Actually I've had a change of mind, Issy. I want to drop the case.'

'Yeah right,' I laughed.

'Honestly, I'm serious.'

If I knew Fiona, and believe me I knew Fiona, there was no way in a million years she'd ditch a case just like that. There had to be a reason. Most probably she was testing my mettle, my dedication.

'After all my hard work?'

'I've made my mind up, Brodsky.'

I was amazed. 'What about the evidence I have?'

'Bin it. I'll explain when we're back in London.'

Stunned that all I'd done was for nought, all the hours spent schmoozing Lisa rendered futile, the compromising kiss, the numerous afternoons spent buddying up in her bedroom, massaging her, brushing her hair, shaving her legs: I felt justifiably goosed.

'Fiona, I can't accept that, I deserve at least a reason.'

'Geraldine and I, we go back a long way and . . . It's personal. Okay, Issy? It's personal,' her tone turned prickly.

Ohh, pardon me for touching a raw nerve.

'It's Nadia's hen party. I want us to enjoy the next few days without incident. Is that okay with you, Issy?'

'Sure, you're the boss, whatever you say goes,' I sighed, so clearly but a minion. Having invested a lot of my 'self' into the case, I took its abandonment personally. However, the up side meant there was one less thing for me to worry about.

I couldn't wait to see the Trap girls and had long forgiven them their daily irritations. My heart even warmed to the thought of a gossip with Trisha. The Honey hen itinerary began with a quick welcome drink followed by one of the more successful Festival shows before coming to view our late-night offering.

AVANTI

'I'm through to the next round of auditions for *The Parlour*,' Lisa casually mentioned on our way to the hotel to meet them all.

187

'Fantastic,' I gasped. 'Guess it was worth the shag, then.'

'No thanks to the Casting Agent. He's been sacked. Seems he was Nell Tony's toyboy until she got wind of his casting methods,' Lisa informed me. 'And I wasn't the only one. What a dog. Oh, Isabel, I need another favour.'

'You're going to be on TV,' I said, awe-inspired. 'You're going to be a star, Lisa.'

'I know. About tonight, would you mind cutting your set back?'

I balked. 'What?'

'Not so much cutting it as sticking to your best three minutes.'

'That is cutting it. Why?'

Five minutes prior to meeting the Honeys at their hotel, Lisa informed me that a journalist from the *Scotsman* and a comedy-show judge had booked tickets for that evening's performance. My jaw dropped; alas, no words came out.

'Geraldine warned me not to tell you in case it made you nervous.'

Nervous? My adrenalin shot into overdrive; I was on the verge of imploding. Dry-mouthed, I gulped.

'You are not serious?'

She swore she was.

It didn't bear thinking about. Christ, the expectations, people whose opinions could have an impact on one's future.

'Are you sure, Lisa?'
'One hundred per cent.'

Lordy, but the pressure was on. I had a quick beer with the Trappiste girls, a slight giggle, a swift catch-up, but I was only half there. My mind had already wandered back to the Royal Mile, the aim being to pack out the house. Worst thing envisaged would be to spot the reviewers in the audience, scribbling away in their notebooks of judgment. There was no way I was going to blow it this time, nor was I going to cut my set short. The Mingers blasted me for even considering it an option. 'That Lisa has an audacity. Issy, you've every right to be here, sure you're miles funnier than she is.'

I WAS FOCUSING, FOCUSING . . .

G-Man, it's me, Issy, just checking in. This time I'm really going for it. No holding back, here's to whatever happens, so say a little a prayer, eh?
    'Issy who are you talking to?'
    'No one, just mumbling my lines.' We stood at the back of the Caves, the four of us platzing, psyching ourselves up. Lisa nudged me in the ribs and winked.
    'Remember, keep it to your best three minutes.'
    'I'll try, Lisa. Can't promise, though.'
    Yeah, right, like I'd let down myself or my comrades-in-arms, especially considering they'd travelled

all the way from London with a huge banner. An enormous banner with my name emblazoned on it, and they were sitting in the front row chanting.

The house lights went down, the house lights came up. Adrian was on stage, warming up the audience.

'Ladies and gentlemen, sit back and enjoy, for tonight I give to you, the one, the only, a close personal showbiz friend of mine, little Issy Brodsky!'

I inhaled a deep, slow breath, then like a small, raucous rebellion, rushed up on to the stage and . . .

STORMED IT

This was like the word dying but it began with fl. I was flying. Hit by a rush of the positive, I swear I nearly fainted. Everything fell into place, the audience was completely behind me, albeit in front of me . . . you get my gist. For the first time ever, I no longer perceived the crowd as sitting in judgment, but more as a willing accomplice or, indeed, a friend's one-year-old. (A young toddler dropped round mine whom I had to win over by making a complete tit out of myself. Tut, tut, reader, and I know what you're thinking, I just didn't think it had to be spelt out.)

That's the comedy juxtaposition. See, it takes a certain amount of confidence to act like an utter twat. No longer scared, I played with the crowd, looking straight back at them as if conducting an orchestra of laughter. My routine flowed, it breathed, each gag like an original thought spilling out of my mouth. I was totally in the moment and halfway through the set my eyes, accustomed to the dark, spotted my number-one choice and, just as I was about to break into my Meat Loaf love ballad, I stalled. Usually the reactions garnered from the random bloke or lady I serenaded were of mortal embarrassment. They would cast their eyes downward, groan or grimace and when I screeched out the line, 'Will you love me forever?' predominantly they'd reply in the negative.

But on this night?

Why was this night different from all other nights?

On this night I took the microphone into the audience and made straight for my number-one choice. I performed the routine and Jake Vincent, to my astonishment, not only knew the words, but joined me in a duet. Together we gave a flawless, though tuneless rendition of 'Paradise by the Dashboard Light'. The audience went ballistic, we got a huge cheer and I milked it like a big fat Hereford. At the end I gave Jake a cheeky elbow nudge, told him if he played his cards right he'd be on to a promise.

And from there on in it just got better.

Sure, I'd experienced good gigs before, but this was different. I'd made a room full of people laugh as a cohesive group, not merely smatterings of chuckles here and there. Then, all too soon, it was over. High-five hand-slapping when I ran off the stage and I felt so happy, happier than I had in a very long time.

Ranking as one of the best moments in my life, it even surpassed that fifteen-minute tantric orgasm I'd shared with a guy in Thailand many, many bare-faced moons ago. I swear I could have surfed the audience. Trisha, Fiona and Nads were freaking out, punching the air, slapping my back, promising me a raise.

*   *   *

Theoretically, the mere action of an audience member making direct eye contact with you, 'the artist', constitutes a measure of approval; add a smile and it's a compliment of your talent; a verbal affirmation or two licks the ego nicely. Next come offers of drinks and by this stage it's you who's laughing, or sipping. What can I say, but the congratulations fell like autumn leaves and, as it was a blue-moon occasion, I enjoyed raking them in.

'You were fantastic. Drink?'

'Sure, that would be great.'

'Loved your set. What you drinking?'

'Anything, cheers.'

'Good stuff. Fab act. Fancy a drink?'

'Thanks.'

'Nice one Issy, get that down you.'

'Tequila!'

'A swifty?'

'Schure.'

'You on for another?'

A nod.

'One for the road?'

A grunt.

A mimed hand signal that taken out of context could be interpreted as a very rude gesture but in this instance meant 'another', answered by an abrupt mirroring gesticulation resembling the tossing of salt over my right shoulder.

193

'Your place or mine?'

'Shorry, I'm a coeliac.'

SOME PEOPLE LET SUCCESS GO TO THEIR HEADS

I was one of those people. My head was at least three or four times its normal size. The Honeys revelled a while, but left before the party really got going, which wasn't till about three in the morning. And as for Lisa?

Poor Lisa, her act had gone okay, but fizzled out at the end. She was in a very nasty mood.

'Dhon't whorry, Lisa, everyone has shit gigs!'

'Fuck off. I asked you to keep to your best three. Thanks to you and the Mingers, I had hardly any time to perform my set. You're so selfish.'

'Shhanks.'

She didn't stay till the bitter end and ran off back to her sugar mummy, Geraldine, who had failed to show up for the performance due to a migraine. Alcoholically diluted, I was saved by the bell-ow of the Mingers.

'Issy! Here! Now!' They slapped an arm around each of my shoulders and we ended up doing some Russian dancing in the Cave bar. I vaguely recall it started out as the can-can but somehow our centre of gravity just kept sinking lower and lower.

*   *   *

Oh, what a night, what a night it was. The Mingers, Adrian and I danced into the morning, then into a newsagent's and bought three copies of the *Scotsman*. First thing to strike us was the stars awarded.

Four glowing pointy yellow stars. Ah, how euphoria kissed us, and conga-style we danced around Bristo Square. We high-kicked it all the way to an all-night pub, came to a halting stance and then purchased a bottle of Champagne.

'Four stars, what d'you reckon, like?'

'F-ing brilliant, he loved it, he loved the show.'

The cork popped and Adrian began to read out the review. 'Titter Club, blah blah, Caves II, blah blah blah, four fresh, talented women strut their stuff, blah blah, and first up was the . . .

. . . Excellent Issy Brodsky.'

'Read it again Adrian,' I cried.

'The Excellent Issy Brodsky.'

'Damn it, Ade, but I can't hear you.'

'The Excellent Issy Brodsky.'

'Come on, my friend, this time with feeling.'

'*The Excellent Issy Brodsky.*'

'And again for all the doubters along the way.'

'The Excellent Issy Brodsky.'

'And one more time, just for the record.'

'The Excellent Issy Brodsky.'

'And for the sake of the near-sighted.'

'The Excellent Issy Brodsky.'

'And for the far-sighted.'

'The Excellent Issy Brodsky.'

And for those who wanted to buy the book, picked it up, but foolishly put it down again.

Ha ha ha . . .

We danced and drank our way back to Lemming Terrace, then collapsed to fade-out.

ALL CHANGE

'Hello?'

'Hello?'

It was way too early to get up. It was blinkety-blink, five o'clock – in the afternoon. Way too early.

Cripes, it was five o'clock in the afternoon. I had turned into a nocturnal being. My mobile was ringing, instinctively I'd reached for it.

'Issy!'

Voice recognition was giving me the 'Geraldine' reading. She said she wanted to meet me at Monster Mash on Forrest Road for tea.

A COUPLE OF HOURS LATER . . .

Pushing open the door to the café, I was expecting to find a woman in remission who would heap upon me accolades and high praise. Ah, how so often our expectations go unmet.

'Issy?'

Oh my . . .

She was right in front of me, staring up at me. To all intents and purposes she was Geraldine, though at the same time she was not, and appeared as a version of her former self. I'm not talking headscarf, wig or bald head.

The Geraldine of yore had a face of character, let's say 'well lived-in'. The change was almost too bizarre for words. How had cancer done this? Immediately it dawned. It hadn't. I was wrong. Geraldine wasn't prone to some life-threatening disease coursing through her bloodstream. The only illness she'd been struck by was age.

Oh the pressures, the pressures of being a woman. The skin on her face had been pulled back to creaseless perfection, her forehead smoothed out, her eyes up-lifted, mouth fish-lipped, teeth whitened. She looked like a freak.

'I thought you were dying.'

'Why would you think that?'

'Cancer, chemotherapy, I thought . . .'

Her lips moved slowly upwards. Smiling looked painful. I winced and wondered whether her skin, like a new pair of leather shoes, would ease out over time.

'You look . . . you look so . . .' The word in mind was outrageous as opposed to the blatant lie I gushed with excessive feeling, 'so much younger.'

Except Geraldine did not look younger in the slightest. She looked like a woman who had had major cosmetic surgery on her face.

'Sit down, Issy.' I slipped into the booth.

'Lisa came clean. I know everything.'

'Excuse me?'

'I know what happened between you and her.'

'Nothing happened.'

She crossed her arms, was staring me down. 'Come now, everyone's saying you haven't let Lisa out of your sight for the past three weeks.'

I flatly denied any wrongdoing. She kept pressing me, was convinced I had seduced 'her Lisa', and deemed me wholly responsible for Lisa's corruption. It always amazed me how most people were blind to their partner's misdeeds. Time after time I'd witnessed it, the idea of infidelity being latent yet so abhorrent to the wronged party that when the penny dropped, when the alarm bell rang, when the neon sign lit up overhead, spelling it out in lurid, fluorescent capital letters, still they refused to believe it. Inevitably they would then seek to blame any thing or person other than their own partner. The partner would then be absolved from the equation, deemed incapable of initiating any transgression. The wicked temptress blamed and suitably punished. I'd seen it a million times before. Geraldine was hurting, thus it was only logical to point the finger in my direction and accuse me of moral corruption.

'From the outset Lisa warned me not to award you a

place in the show. Too late for that, but I've come to a decision.'

'What do you mean?'

'We're dropping you.'

'What? Geraldine, we got four stars in the *Scotsman*. I got a rave review! You can't drop me from the show. You . . .' my bottom lip began to quiver.

'I'm the producer. I can do what I want.'

'Please don't drop me.' I was gobsmacked.

'You've really disappointed me, Issy.'

I begged, pleaded, appealed to Geraldine to no avail. She wouldn't budge. In the end I opted to go for broke, to spill the beans and tell the truth.

'Geraldine, wise up, Lisa's played you for a fool.' I understood Geraldine's steely calm gaze as an indication to proceed. 'She's using you.' Her totally expressionless face stared back at me as if egging me on. 'You're her meal-ticket, a way for her to achieve her goals.' Geraldine's expression remained stoic. 'Lisa's lying. She's been unfaithful to you and not just with me. Geraldine, I have evidence.' All normal facial reactions were missing. 'She's a cheat, a thief, her material isn't even particularly good. You're making a big mistake.'

I noticed tears seep out over Geraldine's lids and skid down her cheeks. Damn, I'd been thrown by her new-look face, and now realised I'd gone overboard. Just because she couldn't show her feelings didn't mean she didn't have any. The serviettes were the cheap non-absorbent kind. She dabbed at the edges

of her eyes then, fingers to her temples, tried to scrunch
them up as if to alleviate her inner torment.

'Sorry, Geraldine.'

A tiny wounded voice eked out of her mouth.

'You're finished in the comedy world, Issy Brodsky,
and that's a promise.'

GOD DAMN IT ALL

My first reaction was to track Lisa down and metaphorically kill her or at least try to work out why she'd
dropped me in it. I found her packing her bags at the
apartment, on her way to Geraldine's hotel.

'I'm out of the show,' I proclaimed disbelievingly.

Infuriatingly she ignored me.

'Lisa, why did you say anything? Lisa? Answer me!'

She, with the slyest of smiles, sneered across at me then
venomously spat, '*Lisa Armstrong, amusing though her
set felt rushed*. Rushed? Three minutes, Issy.'

'But, you had no reason to confess to anything. I
don't understand.'

'Really? Did you know Geraldine was too upset to
attend the show last night 'cause someone told her I'd
been misbehaving, someone tipped her off?'

'It wasn't me,' I protested.

'Hmm, let me see . . . Ah yes, your "friend", Fiona.'

'Fiona? What about Nell? Crispin? The Casting
Agent?'

'I doubt it. Come to think of it, for some reason Fiona's never liked me.'

'Fiona's jealous of you. She's in love with Geraldine,' I explained.

'Exactly, Issy. Fiona had to be getting this information from somewhere.' Jesus Christ. I realised that Fiona must have said something. 'It didn't take a genius to work it out. Ha! Issy Brodsky, a private detective.' She sniggered with glee while my mind whirred, grasping the fact that Fiona would have known she was going to land me in it. So that was why she was eager to close the case.

'I never wanted you in the show, Issy. If Brillo Boy hadn't pulled out . . .'

'Excuse me?'

'You were fourth in line and got lucky.'

'What?'

'Why should I jeopardise everything I've worked hard to achieve for your success, Issy? You very nearly fucked everything up for me.'

'Lisa, this is crazy.'

'Issy, you're a loser, so second rate. You're a second-rate comic, detective, oh yeah, I nearly forgot, and mother.'

You had to hand it to her, Lisa was very good at human reduction, slicing me down to size in one foul swipe. Finally it dawned on me: Lisa Slater, a manipulative operator if ever there was one, was jealous of me (of me!).

'You don't look so *excellent* now, Issy.'

To be honest I didn't feel so great. I felt as if I'd been played by both Lisa and Fiona, the innocent messenger shot down in their game of love. Teeth clenched in rage, I stormed off to hunt down Fiona and have it out with her. I cornered the three Honeys in the hotel lobby on their way to another show.

My face was flushed with fury. I bellowed across at them, 'Geraldine's sacked me!'

Completely taken unawares, Fiona feigned ignorance. 'What did you do this time?'

'What did *I* do? It's what *you* did, Fiona. You grassed me up.'

'I didn't.'

'My own boss blew my cover. How could you shaft me?'

'This is ridiculous, Issy.'

'Fiona, I'm out of the show.'

'Geraldine will come to her senses.'

'What are you not getting? Geraldine is in love with Lisa, she's not interested in you, and never will be.'

Fiona laughed, she was laughing at me, right at me.

'You are such a bitch.'

'Easy, Issy.' Trisha stepped in between Fiona and me.

My, my, Issy but what big hands you've got.
All the better to strangle you, Fiona.
And what big arms you've got.
All the better to crush you.
And what big legs you've got.
All the better to kick you to death.

202

'Issy you've got it wrong,' she stuttered, 'you're wrong. Look, if it wasn't for me, you wouldn't have got the part in the first place.'

That did it, that was the tipping point, the final straw.

'Turns out I won that part!' I've never considered myself a violent person, but I went for her, fists flailing awkwardly. I scuffled my boss to the ground and would have beaten her to a pulp, only Trisha pulled me off.

'Brodsky, you're, you're . . .'

'What, Fiona?' and such was my vehemence I finished the sentence for her. 'Sacked? Big deal.'

And then, well, then I found myself wrapped in Nadia's arms sobbing my heart out. I couldn't contain myself any longer, went to pieces in her hotel room.

'Nads, why do these things always happen to me? Why?'

Her voice was soothing and calming. 'I don't know, Issy.'

MY SACKING?

I don't wish to talk about it. In the larger scheme of disasters I found myself faced with, it was but a niggling pimple on the tip of my nose aching to be squeezed yet not entirely ready.

You can't make me talk about it.

At that point in my psyche I was numb, verging on catatonic.

La la la, but I'll tell you one thing, never ever trust a detective – they are full of deceit.

At noon the next day Nadia and I walked over to the Caves to pick up my nurse's uniform. It was odd to see the venue during daylight hours because, as our show was on so late, I never usually went there. I didn't know any of the daylight-hour front-of-house crew and was very surprised when one approached me with a big bouquet of flowers.

Nadia nudged me. 'What did I tell you, Issy? Looks like they've realised what a mistake they've made.'

'You're one of the Titters aren't you?'

'Was,' I snivelled.

'Oh. Could you give this to Issy Brodsky?'

'I am Issy,' I replied, shocked to have received such a beautiful bunch.

He looked at me like I had two heads. 'I thought the girl with the blonde hair was Issy?'

'You mean Lisa.'

'But I always give her the bouquets.'

'Yep, she's the one with the secret admirers.'

'You're winding me up, right? You can't be Issy Brodsky.'

'I am she,' though, believe me, there were times I wished I wasn't.

'But that would mean . . .'

So warped was Lisa she'd even stolen my secret admirer. There must have been at least a dozen bunches sent over the course of the show. It slotted into place now. Lisa was always the first up at the Caves to sort out the comps and always vague regarding who her admirer was.

'Can you believe this, Nadia? How vile is this woman? I mean, maybe this business isn't for me, maybe this is a sign.'

'Is there a note?'

The note was cryptic: 'Not long now, my love.' Flummoxed as to their origin, it gave me a legitimate reason to call Scarface.

'Hi, Issy,' he droned, his voice flat as he answered the phone. 'Things getting any better for you?'

'Yes and no,' I replied, 'how about you?'

'Fine. Perhaps I should tell you, I'm seeing someone.'

'Oh, right. Congrats,' I flinched. 'I take it it's not you who's been sending me all those bouquets of flowers then.'

'Eh, no.'

'Great,' I cheered. 'I was hoping it wasn't. Just had to double check. Bye.' Bastard, I mumbled under my breath and then rang Max. He also denied sending anything, 'No way, Mum,' and then my mother reminded me they were due to arrive at the end of the week.

How strange, I thought, to have such a dedicated admirer, but who could it be? My imagination went overboard on the most romantic of fantasies; by some weird twist of fate it would turn out to be Jan or perhaps even my number-one choice. Maybe my mother was right in advising me to quit my desperate search for Mr Right and let him find me.

'Nads,' I said, feeling the happiest I had in the past twenty-four hours, 'this could be my silver lining. I mean, he's clearly loaded. Maybe he's famous and that's why he hasn't signed his name. I have a strong feeling about this one, he's definitely coming to get me.'

YES, HE WAS DEFINITELY COMING TO GET ME

And then it struck, the realisation, my secret fan, unknown devotee, green-fingered enthusiast, jeez, but I could see the headlines, a dose of double duping for Double D undercover agent, Issy Brodsky . . .

Click, click, like an osteopath at work, it suddenly fell into place. The *thing* I wasn't to worry about. That minor nuisance I had relegated to the pending pile. The communication link Bambuss had been talking about.

Eureka!

The one-time gardener of Arthur Penn, or rather his alias, Darren.

In retrospect, Lisa did me a favour leaving me blissfully unaware of the potential danger I was in. If I'd known, I certainly wouldn't have stayed in Edinburgh. I would have freaked, as I then did, almost gagging on the fear.

Bambuss was on the case in a flash, the tracing of the flower shop instigated, the card given over to forensics and himself flown up that very night. Before last orders he was down the Oxford Bar. All the staff from the Caves were interviewed, Lisa too. I would have pressed charges for flower theft, but Lisa gave a flawless performance. She claimed total innocence and blamed the front-of-house guy for assuming she was I. This, she attested, was reaffirmed, as none of the notes accompanying the bouquets, which of course she could not produce, had named me. She believed the bouquets were intended for her and offered her profuse apologies. Bambuss fell for it hook, line and sinker. I was disappointed, as I had hoped to use her theft as a bargaining tool to get myself reinstated and back on the show. In the end, though, I didn't have to. Bambuss ordered my reinstatement, declaring me 'Darrenbait' for the rest of the run. Reluctantly Geraldine accepted this, with the proviso being I stay well clear of Lisa.

That, I assured her, she didn't have to worry about.

What I did worry about, though, was the discovery that the flowers had been hand-delivered every day, at the same time, by the same man, which dictated that Darren had been following me for ages.

'You mean . . .'

'Yes,' Bambuss decreed, suitably melodramatic in tone. 'He's here, probably has been since the beginning.'

So there we were, three Honeys, one ex-Honey (me) and Bambuss sitting in a police interview room, drinking sweet tea and eating dry, day-old Danish pastries.

The atmosphere was highly toxic, notwithstanding the fact that twenty-four hours earlier I'd lunged at Fiona.

Bambuss was talking about working together as a team, striving for a common goal, nailing the bastard and ripping him apart. 'Brodsky, think of all the people you've encountered since the show began. It's highly probable you've met him and spoken to him.'

All the people? Christ, I'd approached hundreds of the species on a daily basis trying to offload tickets as I traipsed the Royal Mile. I'd encountered more people over three weeks in Edinburgh than I had in the past ten years.

'Think, Brodsky, as a detective would.'

'Ex-detective,' Fiona put in.

Agh, such fond memories I had of that day job.

THE DAY JOB

The speed with which events unfolded left me panting. Fiona disappeared back to London in a huff, Trisha left me a marked envelope, then followed suit. It looked far too ominous and official to open immediately, so I stuffed it down into the nether regions of my bag. Nadia promised to stay glued to my side till something occurred and Bambuss instructed me to continue on as if nothing had happened.

As if!

So there we were, Nads and I back at Lemming Terrace. Following Lisa's evacuation to the hotel, her room was now empty, though filthy. I took advantage. Quitting my solitary cell, and with scrubbing bucket in hand, I set to cleaning. It didn't take long before I unearthed the 'lost' cards under the wardrobe, together with a dirty thong.

Twelve cryptic messages, in BIC's Biro blue. Nads had only just gotten round to reading *The Da Vinci Code*, so she was in her element, determined on deciphering the meanings. The least cryptic one was: *In recognition of your first death. Here's to the next.*

'Issy, he saw your death performance,' gasped Nadia.

'What an awful night that was,' I glumly replied.

'Well, remember anything strange, anyone unusual?'

'Nads, I was out of my skull. You'd be better off asking Adrian.'

Adrian and the Mingers were in recovery from some post-coital experience and tucking into a greasy Chinese. Their reaction to my sacking, reinstatement and role of psychopathic bait was one of bewildered incredulity. As regards Lisa, they kept saying, 'We told you that Lisa was lethal. Everyone knows she's a walking perversion, sure, she stole your best jokes. She kept putting you down all the time. We thought you were a right arsehole, Issy.'

Wow, top that for a vote of confidence.

At Nadia's behest, Adrian, chomping through his chow mein, contemplated the night of my death. 'You were all over the place that night, though you did talk to the bloke from across the road, you definitely spoke to him for a bit.'

'What bloke?'

'He came up to you after the show. Academic looking, heavy beard, thick glasses.'

I vaguely recalled a bearded bloke. 'You mean . . . What? Not the one who said I should stick to my day job?'

'Very same, I saw him today in the local deli.'

I shuddered, a fearsome chill swept through my body. 'Adrian, what was he buying?'

'Dunno.'

'Come on, think.'

Adrian glared at me like I'd asked the most stupid question. 'Eh, pâté? Cuddly toys? I dunno.'

I glowered back, demanding his concentration by pointing my Maglite key ring in his face.

'Eh, herrings, that was it.'

'Herrings. You sure?'

Adrian nodded.

'Nads, get Bambuss on the phone, pronto.'

HE SHALL HAVE A FISHY ON A LITTLE DISHY, HE SHALL HAVE A FISHY WHEN THE BOAT COMES IN

Reader, I know what you're thinking: No way! How neat would that be? But think of all the movies you've seen where the psycho lives within spitting distance of the would-be victim, or actually in the same building. It's practically mandatory. All whacko doppelgangers worth their psycho salt can be found within spitting distance of their desired victims. I ask you, why should my psycho be different from anyone else's?

Within the hour, there was a swoop on the house directly across the road from ours. Darren emerged handcuffed, with Bambuss marching triumphantly beside him, behind them were a handful of trigger-happy terrorist police in full combat gear, to their left side were a couple of coppers, to the right side stood Mrs Nesbit, Gordon McCracken and Dilys from the corner shop, gossiping at a tremendous rate. I looked down on the unfolding scene from the safety of the kitchen window. Darren stopped at the gate, his blood-curdling gaze turned upward and menacing eyes locked on mine. Slowly and inelegantly he licked his lips and then started shouting, 'This isn't the end, Issy Brodsky! I'll have you yet.'

'What?' I cried out, terrified.

'He said he'd have you yet,' repeated Minger Two.

'You and I, we're just beginning.' He smiled up at me inanely. 'Mark my words, Issy Brodsky.'

'What?' I gasped in horror.

'He said . . .'

'I know what he said, Minger! Jesus Christ, can someone close this window!' Below, Bambuss tugged at Darren's arm while he remained glued to the spot.

'We, Brodsky, have a lot in common, you and I . . .'
His voice was gruff and he enunciated every letter in
my name and then compared me to the following,
'Judas, Lucifer, Spawn of Satan, Beelzebub, Simon
Cowell. May the curse of . . .'

Mercifully, at this juncture Adrian managed to lower the sash window and drown out his spine-chilling
threat, coinciding with Bambuss walloping him on the
side of his head. The last I heard of Darren was,
'Owwwwwwwwwww!'

'You okay, Issy?' Nadia asked.

'Sure,' I replied. My focus remained fixed. I saw a fat
slug innocently loitering on the pavement fall victim to
the underside of a little girl's pink Adidas flashing
trainers.

'Christ, are you not totally freaked?' Minger One
enquired.

'I feel sorry for Darren, to tell the truth,' I mumbled
half-heartedly. A gust of wind blew Mrs Nesbit's
hemline northward and revealed her left knee for a
split second, but time enough for Gordon McCracken
to file it in his memory. A glimpse of such a knee was a
profound moment indeed. He breathed in deeply and
lingered on the image.

'Issy?' yelped Minger Two. 'You positive you're
okay, like?'

A spider, as if on pointes, moved across the lilac-
painted wall and a bluebottle came to a buzzing halt at
the base of the window.

'Issy . . .'

I smacked my closed fist down on to the fly and squashed him dead. 'Huh, Adrian?' I yawned.

'Do you want a cup of sweet tea?'

'JUST MY USUAL, PLEASE'

Back at my favourite, Café Blunt, I was in a mulling state, having waved Nadia off on the train back to London. By rights I should have been picking up my wee man and my parents but, due to psycho Darren, they cancelled their trip. Max was really disappointed, but much cheered when instead they surprised him with a trip to Euro Disney. It was, in the circumstances, the correct decision. My Edinburgh existence was as far removed from the daily routine of motherhood as it could possibly get, my work hours were still firmly rooted in the nocturnal world and there was no doubt that if Max had come up, he would have found it frustrating to stay with my parents and see me for just a couple of hours in the afternoon.

We were nearing the end of the Festival. The fizz was petering out, audiences running dry and our enthusiasm dampened. For most performers total exhaustion had begun to set in after nearly a month's hard work and harder play. I barely saw Lisa – she'd turn up at the Caves halfway through the Mingers' set, avoid all eye contact and then disappear straight after the show.

'How's the show going?' chirped the friendly waitress handing me my usual.

'Nearly over.' I tried not to sound too suicidal.

'Never mind, there's always next year.'

Not if Geraldine had anything to do with it. It forcibly struck me that I would be returning to London without a job or a (comedy) career to speak of. From Heathrow it would be straight back to Belsize Park and the job section of the *Camden New Journal* or *Ham & High*. Yep, my immediate future didn't look so super-shiny. In fact it looked pretty darned bleak. Guess it was time for another career move, though in which direction, I hadn't a clue. If the worst came to the worst, I suspected I could always do another course. Indeed, all things considered, I'd probably have to do another course. Maybe something like counselling – I'd be good at that, able to relate to others' misery – or maybe interior design. There was always the café at the end of road. Come to think of it, waitressing had tided me over before. Silvio was always asking me to come back. He'd promised to up my rate by 50p an hour, which may I add, was getting perilously close to the minimum wage.

'Great news, Issy.' The Mingers had turned up full of the joys of Adrian and snapped me out of my self-absorbed glumness by announcing, 'We all have tickets!'

'Tickets? To what?'

'Call yourself a comedian? It's the Awards tonight.'

*   *   *

The if.commedies, or Eddies, were to comedians what the Oscars were to movie stars, or perhaps more appropriately, the Mercury Music Awards to musicians. Anyway, they were a massive deal. If you did manage to win one, it's hello telly series and bye-bye humdrum reality. Post-awards was the party, which was pretty much the highlight of the Festival's social calendar, in that there was a meagre chance you'd be turned away if you weren't on the list.

So, wearing my best smile and with our golden tickets, the Mingers, Adrian and I arrived straight after our show. It was a shabby-glam affair, nothing too spectacular, but anyone who was anyone was there.

I left my coat in the cloakroom and was immediately accosted by the high, rising decibels of Crispin the ACTOR, master of articulation and pronunciation.

'Four stars, Brodsky. Not bad for a beginner.' He was looking his ultra-cute self. 'What you drinking? Four Star? Crap joke, I'm pissed Lizzy . . . Issy, sorry. Come over here, come meet my crew.'

I followed a dangling bottle of Champagne to the far side of the room, where a small group of people were arguing about human trafficking and how crap their so-called agents were at getting them auditions and there, amongst them all, sat Jan. Damn, but in retrospect it was so clear. The night of my death, Jan had been sitting beside none other than Crispin. How could I have forgotten the first rule of detecting, which is to revisit the scene, have a good old nose and then follow up on all leads? I hadn't followed up on the most obvious of all leads (or any, actually. Look, I'd been really busy with Darren and Lisa and all that).

When I clapped eyes on Jan, my heart flipped, then pounded with such ferocity I thought it was going to rip itself from out of my chest, throw itself on the floor and pulsate at his feet.

'Bugger them all,' bellowed Crispin and introduced me. 'This here is the wonderfully talented Isabel Brodsky . . .' I went all coy, flattered by his compliments. '. . . whom the *Scotsman* branded a very good comedienne.'

'Actually it was "excellent",' I corrected him.

'My mistake, "excellent". Our show unfortunately was written off as worse than a care-in-the-community project.' Crispin swung round to Jan, 'Jan, remember that female comedy show we went to see . . .'

He looked at me blankly, 'No, sorry.' Well, at least he didn't remember me from the death show.

'Drink?' asked Jan.

My face was splashed a putrid red. I could barely meet his gaze. He cocked his head to one side. 'Yes or no?'

'Yeah, okay, thanks,' I gabbled and let him fill my glass.

'I'm Jan by the way.'

'I know,' I replied, wondering how it was that he did not recognise me. Had I really aged so badly? How

216

bizarre that two people should meet and the impact for one was life-changing yet for the other bore no significant relevance? It was then I took a deep breath, prepared myself and very quietly prodded his memory.

'I'm Issy . . . Isabel . . . we met about six years ago, at Glastonb . . .' The hardest sentence I'd ever had to stutter/mutter.

'Issy! Glastonbury. Of course! Issy!' His face lit up. 'I knew it! I so knew it. I kept looking at you, you look so familiar.'

He knew it. Of course he knew it. Of course he recognised me. How could I have doubted he wouldn't?

'Dizzy Issy.' Hand slapped to forehead, in his wildest dreams he couldn't believe it, the shock appeared genuine.

'I know . . . I've changed,' I explained.

'A bit. But Glastonbury, with Issy . . .' He ran his fingers through his fair locks. The conversation faltered then rattled on staccato-style before he said, 'Where did you disappear to?'

'Into the crowd.'

'You never gave me your number . . .'

I took a seat, a drink, another and soon my nervousness subsided. Jan was sexy, very good-looking in a pretty-boy way, though he knew it. He kept tossing his hair to the side and giving me a certain 'look', undoubtedly mirror-practised and probably in usage since adolescence.

And I swore to myself that no matter how drunk I

got, I would not blurt a word about him being the father of my son. For once I aimed to play it cool and avoid foolishly rushing in.

'Issy, Crazy Issy,' and reminiscing, he smiled. 'Remember that weekend? I should have taken your number. Why didn't I take your number?'

At the time I'd been going through a fatalistic period, leaving all in the lap of the cosmos. 'Guess I should have given it to you,' I replied. Of course, at the time, I was also going out with Finn. Poor Finn. I heard recently through the grapevine that his wife was expecting twins. Poor, poor Finn.

'Wanna dance?'

We pushed our way through the crowd, towards the huge sweeping staircase. On the top step about to descend – and no, reader, I didn't trip – no *Sesame Street* 'baker falling with his cakes' skit.[1] Not a bit of it, see what happened was Jan stopped to chat with a friend and was momentarily pulled aside. So alone, top step, mid-staircase I teetered, dividing the upward stream of people when . . .

Eye-lock alert.

Eye-lock alert.

My number-one choice came bounding up the stairs, straight towards me, wearing a black suit jacket over a t-shirt and a pair of jeans. Stopping on the step directly below mine, he looked up into my face and declared, 'Sorry, I'm late.'

1 Christ, I love that skit, it gets me every time.

Dear oh dear, but wasn't it always the way? Never rains but buckets. I shook my head in mock disdain, folded my arms. 'See, if there's one thing I can't bear it's tardiness,' I flirted.

'How about tidiness?'

'No tidiness is, well, close to Godliness.'

'I'm a very spiritual man,' Jake stated.

'I could see that in your ascension.'

His eyes sparkled. 'Are you . . .?'

Jan grabbed me from behind, wrapped his arms round my waist, nuzzled my ear.

'Otherwise engaged I see.' Jake Vincent stepped aside to let the pair of us descend. Damn it, but during those few exchanges my heart had gone giddy-up, our verbal challenges, teasing flirtations, my neck craned back for a final parting glance. Jake Vincent scowled at me, so I stuck out my tongue.

Jan yanked my arm and I followed my Dutchman down the stairs, on to the dance floor. The DJ was playing a tune whose lyrics sounded like 'Remember me, I'm the one who had your baby.' I couldn't help but laugh.

Beneath the mirrorball we moved from tango to waltzing to grinding to disco, attempting each step with varying degrees of success. And then Jan cupped my face in his hands and we stopped moving and he kissed me. Full on the lips and he kissed me and again he kissed me and there are kisses and then there are KISSES and perhaps it was pheromonal, human, chemical, it was most definitely chemical . . .

*   *   *

219

I was overdosing on happiness.

Jan had a flat in one of the nicer Edinburgh hoods. It was huge, spacious, clean.

'I can't believe I met you again,' he whispered.

'Me neither,' I replied staring deep into his eyes. Part of me was scared, expectations of past times lay on the horizon. It could never live up to my memories of Glastonbury, yet the other part of me was feeling sluttish. I mean, I had my reputation to consider. Did I really want to go home a Festival virgin? Peer pressure was getting to me. Physically we connected. How naff would it be not to, at the very least have tried?

Jan slumped on to the sofa and pulled me down with him.

And the light went click.

Some things are best left unturned, like stones, or in the dark, like ugly people, or out, like painfully cringey sex scenes in novels – it can go either way, cold and pornographic or Mills & Boon fairytale floral-scented tripe. I bow out to your imagination, reader. (Wow, that was good, you dirty, dirty reader you!) And then the light went on again. The mood changed, shifted dramatically. For one, the light was piercing. I squinted, pulling the covers up over me. With a groan, Jan stopped midway . . . 'Sorry Issy, I can't.' As if struck by a guilty conscience, he fell away from me and lay back down on the pillows.

'What do you mean you can't?' I thought he was joking – he very clearly could.

'I . . . it's . . . Can I tell you something?'

'Sure,' I sighed, disappointed.

'I really fell for you that weekend,' he smiled.

'Did you?'

'It was intense, what we had.'

I nodded, 'I'm so glad you said that . . .'

He interrupted me.

'My girlfriend's pregnant.'

When Trisha left Edinburgh she handed me an envelope. The scary envelope that I was loath to open. It contained more than my expected P45. It contained the following information.

Jan de Groot
Born 1975, eldest of three children to Lucia and Dieter de Groot. Father, deceased, was a furniture designer, a master craftsman – the de Groot plastic chair is considered one of the most innovative pieces of the '70s and made a fortune, which he subsequently lost to gambling. His mother was a watercolour artist, prone to bouts of depression. He had a bohemian shabby-chic, middle-class upbringing, private schooling, read philosophy at Manchester University and graduated with a third. Spent his twenties drifting between jobs, a stint in the City followed by a year in India, then two

years in Paris working with an avant-garde circus company. He returned to London [which was probably when I met him] and completed a masters at the Webber Douglas Academy drama school. Currently living in Shepherd's Bush in a house with Amelia Davis, an actress and his on/off girlfriend of five years.

'Wow, pregnant.' Trisha had obviously missed that bit out. 'That's fantastic,' I commented.

'Six months. I'm being a jerk,' he said indicating the 'bed', which I interpreted to mean what we were doing in it.

'I guess these things happen.'

'Time to get serious.'

'Yeah,' I nodded, 'having a kid is a big deal.'

'What are you doing?

I had slipped from under the covers and began dressing.

'Where you going?'

'Home.'

'I'm sorry, Issy. I saw a scan of the baby today, she emailed it to me. Our baby. My child.'

'I've a son,' I announced. I had to say something, for Max's sake.

'Really?'

'Yeah.'

'How old is he?' he asked.

'Max is five-and-a-half.' I met Jan's gaze. 'Here, have a look.' I showed him a picture of Max from my mobile phone.

'He's beautiful. I'd no idea you were a mum.'

'I didn't have your number,' I explained.

'Sorry?'

I sat on the edge of the bed. 'You should look after your girlfriend, she needs you right now.'

'Issy, you don't have to go.'

'I do.'

My thoughts had turned to Max and I fused, emotionally short-circuited, feelings of vulnerability clashed with aggressive protection. The infinite depth of love I feel watching Max grow and develop compounded with the unfathomable loneliness that comes from bearing the weight of this responsibility on my own. All the challenges Max had met on his journey. The tiny things, from discovering his toes to discovering shadows, learning to feed himself, getting the spoon into his mouth, then the food on the spoon into his mouth. Communicating with him by way of gestures, then one-syllable words, short sentences to now, learning to read and write. And it didn't stop there, the immeasurable joy Max has brought to my life, the meaning he has given it, even illuminating my own shortcomings as a parent – the times I've lost my temper with him, not to mention the sheer exhaustion and drudgery of child-rearing that had me nearly trounced.

Suppressing the geyser of tears mounting, out I scuttled into the morning. Then, hitting street level, I crumbled, along with those long-clung-to vestiges of nonsensical, mythical daddy scenarios and 'if only' daydreams. My plump, fleshy heart was fissure-torn and a million thoughts of Max fell from my eyes.

HERE COMES MY *FIDDLER ON THE ROOF* MOMENT

Cue the violinist, the one with a splendid sense of balance dancing on the rooftops . . . and God . . .

Well G, got to hand it to you, this time you've really outdone yourself. Wow, I've certainly encountered more than my fair share of crap lately. I mean, where should I start: falling prey to Lisa's manipulation, acting as Fiona's dumb-ass pawn, ending up as Geraldine's excuse for continuing in a rubbish relationship, Darren's paranoia come to life, and now, just for good measure, meeting Jan again and his girlfriend being pregnant all thrown into the mix so casually? Well guess what, G, I'm tired of it. I feel like I'm being hit from every angle, none of which I have any control over. Or maybe that's the point, hey?

Maybe that's the point.

Oh, I get it now, G. It's another of your toughening-up exercises. Well done, Big Man. I feel so very insignificant. Shit, and all along I thought I was just doing my best. Playing the clown, trying to please the crowd, always keeping a happy medium. My mother was right – I have to stop seeking approval. What an idiot. What an idiot. Yet, and here's the rub, weirdly reminiscent of my comedy character. Can't believe it took me so long to work out.

G, I reckon I've got you sussed now, so surprise me.

Go on, I dare you, G, do something unexpected, do something wild.

LONDON, ONE MONTH LATER

'Max,' I roared, 'hurry up or we're going to be late.'

'Coming, Mum,' he cried. 'Just looking at a snail.' A normal ten-minute walk could, at Max's pace, take anything up to an hour, depending on any number of minute pavement distractions. It was frustrating, to say the least.

'Max – now!' I screamed.

'You are so bossy!' he shouted back.

I left my five-year-old son for a month and had, on my return, received a mini-teen. He had a reinforced attitude, a baseball cap and ill-fitting jeans that finished midway across his bottom. Most annoyingly, though, he pretended to be dumb, and unable to register my voice, forcing me to repeat myself over and over.

'Max!'

There I had been, pushing my 'everything but the kitchen sink' suitcase into the arrivals hall, fairly dazed to be back in the land of reality, when a whirlwind force of boy energy almost tackled me to the ground.

225

And I'd looked at him as a stranger would, down at this beautiful little boy.

'Mum!' he smiled and threw his arms around me.

'Who gave you permission to grow so much?' I demanded.

'Mum!' Agh, to be called Mum again. I'd forgotten how lovely it was to be one. 'Mum, I haven't seen you for twenty-eight days . . .'

'Five hours and thirty-four minutes,' I added. 'Come here, Boy Wonder, and give me a big cuddle.'

My parents approached with sheepish grins, Mother acting most coy and wearing lipstick.

'Issy,' my father's voice boomed and he hugged me close to him, 'darling, congratulations are due.'

'Thanks.' I was slightly baffled, unsure whether the congratulations were for surviving Edinburgh or for the review or for just being me.

'Not you,' my father flapped. 'Darling, your mother must have told you?'

'Told me what?'

My mother's smile developed into a peal of giggles. 'Issy, your father and I have something to tell you.'

You guessed it. My mother and father were getting married again. They were bursting with happiness, though how they thought they'd get it right the second time round I had no idea. I suppose I should have been more jubilant, but marriage, well, it was just such a drastic step. I urged them to take it slowly and live in sin for at least a couple of years.

'We're too old to hang around, gotta grab the opportunity.'

'Mum, what about Wally?'

'Your father was right,' my mother acknowledged, throwing her eyes heavenward. 'Wally was always telling me to confront my feelings, let everything out and not fester emotionally. So I told him I had un-resolved feelings for your father, and he went crazy.'

Poor Wally. So much for his New Age, anti-patriarchal new man stance. When my mother came clean, he immediately reverted to type, ie, male and a bastard. He was initiating proceedings, hoping to sue to my mother for breach of their 'Mutual-Respect-4-Infinity' contract, an alternative non-leg-ally-binding relationship document listing out one another's expectations.

'His reaction highlights what a wuss he is,' my mother stated. 'The more he tries to fight me, the more pitiful he appears. Really, Issy, I can't believe you never said anything.'

See, nothing changes – suddenly it was all my fault! Ah, it felt good to be home. We had a celebratory dinner the night of my return. Our entire family came together for the first time since Max's birthday party. Freddie showed up with his boyfriend, sporting matching commitment tattoos. I saw my father bite his tongue, but all in all the evening was a great success. I couldn't stop kissing Max and cuddling him and tickling him. Edinburgh already felt a million miles away, which was bizarre, considering it had only been a matter of hours since I closed the door on a crucial chapter of my life and one of the rankest flats I'd ever had the misfortune to inhabit. Our very last show had been dreadfully anticlimactic, a bit like having sex with Scarface (bitchy, I know, but irresistible). As quickly as the arts world descended on Edinburgh, it lifted like a plague of locusts and by the final night the town had a near-ghostly aura. During that day I'd tried to cram in as many shows as possible, but the best had sold out long in advance and many others had shut up shop. Deflated, I slowly traipsed home in the incessant drizzle, bumping into the Mingers and Adrian on their way to Bristo Square for the comedy cabaret finale.

'Hey, girl, you not coming to the show?'

'Nah, it was sold out. And I've an early flight tomorrow.'

'Shit, right. We probably won't be seeing you then.'

'You all packed, Issy?'

'Pretty much, Sandra.'

Sandra gaped like I'd mooned in her face and Linda gave me a slow clap. Believe me, I was not proud of the fact that it had taken me almost four weeks to work out who was who in the Minger twin-set.

'You're such a one.'

'Get her, what a one.'

Being, 'a one', was high praise indeed coming from the Mingers and I was suitably flattered. I was tempted to brand them a massive number two, but opted for 'pair'. They were 'a right pair'.

We decided traditional farewells were too hazardous.

'No tears, right? It took me ages to put on this muck. Come on, Linda, I don't want to be late.'

They managed to hail a cab and in Sandra climbed.

'Shove your lardy arse that way so's I can fit mine in,' Linda squealed.

Adrian and I were left standing on the pavement.

'Guess that's it, Big A. My first and maybe only Edinburgh.'

'Geraldine will come round . . .'

'You think?' I asked.

He nodded. 'Issy, watching you I saw the faintest glimmer of a star, though shrouded by heavy clouds and millions of light years of distance.'

'Jeez, Adrian, I'm choking up.'

Yes, for all the anxiety, craziness and stress experienced in the past month, Edinburgh had also been one of the most intense periods of my life. I'd indulged in a lifestyle impossible to re-create in London being a working mum. Or, rather, now just a mum.

'MAX!'

He was doing it on purpose, tailing behind. I'd only managed to get him out of the house by allowing him bring his Game Boy.

It had taken a while for Max and me to reacclimatise. Our natural rhythm had been disrupted and it was a few days before we resumed normal relationship services, such as his familiar patter down the hallway and clamber up into my bed, or his arm flung casually round my waist, or a kiss randomly planted on my cheek, or the pair of us cracking up over a smelly fart joke, or him playing while I read the paper, even our familiar bickering, the cheekiness, the heave-ho of routine, or just walking down the road separately yet together, him behind me, then in front, then at my side, a flibbertigibbet, a gibbertiflibbert, bending down to look at ants or pull leaves off trees or climb low walls to walk along, or . . .

'Max,' I repeated, volume raised to the loudest level, 'hurry up, come on!'

His reply a confounding, 'Stop shouting. You are so rude, Mum.'

'Come on or we'll be late for the wedding.'

My feet were killing me: heels, four inches high, sending me off balance, the upper soles pinching, my toes slightly scrunched. Couldn't believe I'd fallen for the old 'don't worry, they will give in time' line.

'Even patent leather?' I'd asked, and the assistant had grinned inanely. 'If you wear them round the house for a few hours, you'll be fine.' I had two blisters before I'd even shut the hall door behind me.

Max was looking exceedingly dapper in his crisp white shirt and black canvas jeans. Thankfully the invitation stated that dress was informal, lounge, black tie optional. Max was already very conscious of his appearance and personal hygiene – a splash of aftershave slapped on his cheeks being a habit picked up from his grandpa and his hair spiked with gel so that his curls were fairly rigid on his head. There we were on a beautiful late summer day at the end of September, the two of us inching ever so slowly up Regent's Park Road on our way to Nadia's wedding. Nads had opted for a civil ceremony and managed to book the grand room in Cecil Sharp House in Primrose Hill.

We met Maria and Bambuss at the gates. Both were deeply tanned and happy. They had just returned from a bargain two-week cruise around the Seychelles.

'Issy!' Bambuss awkwardly grasped my shoulders to bear hug me.

'Detective Bambuss, how was the cruise?'

'Wonderful,' answered Maria, pinching Max's cheek flesh between her thumb and forefinger and then wagging it violently.

Max nearly went ballistic. 'Get off me,' he shrieked.

'Such a big boy,' she chuckled and to add insult to injury ruffled his carefully styled hair. An action that, if administered by myself, would have brought a swift kick to my shins and much sulking. In this instance Max merely snarled and then, incredibly, gave Maria, as ordered, a big Kissie Wissie. For his trouble he was promptly presented with a crisp ten-pound note. Lucky for me he still hadn't grasped the concept of money.

'I'll keep it safe for you, Max,' I suggested and quickly deposited the note in my clutch bag.

'So, Bambuss,' I began, 'first I provide you with the woman of your dreams [if it hadn't been for me those two would never have gotten together] and then hand you your nemesis on a golden plate.' Darren Deacon was, at present, for the safety of the general public, languishing in a high-security prison awaiting trial.

'Indebted, Brodsky.' With a closed fist Bambuss thumped his heart. 'Really, if there is ever anything you or Max need, you just have to ask. We are family now.'

I was flattered and relieved that Bambuss and I had finally laid our chequered past of misunderstanding behind us. 'Any sign of a knighthood?'

He winked. 'I hear it's coming, next time round.'

Trisha arrived with her three teenagers and toyboy. Max was thrilled – there was nothing cooler than playing with an older kid, especially one who was as dedicated/addicted to Game Boy as himself. The usual warnings of 'don't get into any trouble' were issued and off they scampered.

Post-Edinburgh I'd met up with Trisha when I'd called by the office one afternoon to pick up my stuff, return the keys and, on pain of conscience, repay the hours I'd misappropriated. Admit it, you thought I'd forgotten about that money. I hadn't – it niggled at the back of my mind. I'd called in advance to make certain I wouldn't run into Fiona while I was there. She wasn't there and nor, as it happened, was anyone else. I could have waited outside but, as I had the keys, I let myself in.

All my personal bits and bobs had been cleared and

carelessly tossed in an open cardboard box with my name scrawled across it. A quick rummage revealed a paltry testament to my past working life as a Honey: chewed-upon pencils, spot cream, a packet of mints, a miniature cow bell, chipped mug, soluble vitamin-C tablets and a pair of laddered tights. I sat at my old desk, whistled aimlessly awhile, flicked through Fiona's latest issue of *Vogue*, when the phone rang and automatically I reached out to answer it.

'Hi, the Honey Trap, how can I help?'

'Brodsky, is that you?'

'Eh . . . Hi, Fiona. Where are you?'

'Where am I? What the hell are you doing at the office?' She was fuming, steam coming out of the receiver. 'Don't you get it, Brodsky? You're sacked. Put me on to Trisha.'

'Trisha is . . . out, she'll be back in five.'

'And make sure you're gone in five.'

An hour later Trisha walked in. I'd fielded four calls in the meantime and taken on two new potential cases.

'His name is Manny, he's under the impression we're an escort agency and . . .'

'I hope you told him where to go.'

'The thing is, he's a masochist. This could be a runner, Trisha, just torment him with the idea of getting close to being laid but never actually do it. Easy money for a Honey.'

'Brodsky! You're not getting any ideas about being reinstated.'

* * *

The café at the end of my street had been the first port of call on my search for a new job. Unfortunately, it had a full set of waiting staff. Silvio backtracked like nobody's business after having sworn to me that, 'Whenever, whenever Issy, you need a job, you come see Silvio and I sort you out, eh?'

'Trapping and I are over,' I told Trisha, although to be honest I'd only sought to retrieve my box of crap on the premise of begging for my job back. 'Though, Trisha, it has to be said, it's heartening to see the office operating so efficiently in my absence.'

'As you well know, Issy, decent staff are hard to come by.'

It felt like old times: the sarcasm, the kettle put on, the mini street mission to buy some cakes. We sat gabbing the afternoon away, Trisha probing me about Jan. I related the whole sad episode.

'You did right, Brodsky, in the circumstances.'

Considering the circumstances, there was no right or wrong. I'd left Jan with just enough information about Max to draw a conclusion should he wish to. Trisha put her faith in 'Father Time', as opposed to 'Father Hood'. Time, she believed, had the same effect on concentrated emotion as washing-up liquid had on grease. It cut straight through it. I guess at the very least and if the time ever did come, Max could look for him later in life if he chose to.

'How was Fiona with you on the phone?'

234

'Not particularly friendly,' I responded.

'Issy, you do know it wasn't her who dumped you in it.'

'What do you mean?'

'She was pretty shook up when you went for her.'

'Trisha, it had to be Fiona. She was so in love with Geraldine she was bordering on obsessed.'

'Hate more like. Fiona hated Geraldine.'

'What?'

Turned out that for most of senior school Fiona had had a huge crush on Geraldine. A hideous crush of much magnitude and wholly unreciprocated. Geraldine used to call Fiona her shadow boy and looked straight through him.

'Meeting Geraldine again presented a choice opportunity for Fiona to exact revenge. She wanted to humiliate Geraldine,' explained Trisha.

'I thought she was in love. That's awful.' I'd always considered Fiona to be fairly level-headed in matters of the heart.

'Pretty low, I agree, and in the end fruitless.'

See, the more Fiona sought her pound of flesh the more she realised how pathetic she was being. Prior to the hen trip to Edinburgh, Fiona and Geraldine had a cathartic meeting during which Geraldine offloaded years of harboured guilt regarding her appalling treatment of Fiona. Fiona didn't say anything with regards to her own misdeeds, hence stopping the case, and she was hoping no details of Lisa's misbehaviour would come to light.

This information left me stunned. It had to have been Fiona.

'So what's happened between her and Geraldine?'

'Fiona feels dreadful and Geraldine refuses to take her calls.'

'Jesus, Trisha, I was so convinced Fiona grassed me up.'

'Between us, she realises she misled you and her behaviour was shoddy. She felt pretty awful when you were dropped from the show.'

Not as awful as I was beginning to feel. I'd sought out Brillo Boy, the comedienne I'd replaced in the Titter Club, to clarify whether I'd earned my place on merit or if it had been a fix. She told me Fiona had paid her to drop out of the finals of the competition at the very last minute, thus enabling me to take part.

'But you did win it.'

'How do you mean?'

'That night it was down to the audience's votes. You won it, Issy, fair and square.' Well, not quite fair and square – if it hadn't been for Fiona's magnanimous gesture, I wouldn't have had the opportunity.

'So how much did she pay you off?' I asked.

'Fifty quid.'

'That little!' I was appalled.

'In any case, I wouldn't have been able to do the show. I'd been offered a part in *Mamma Mia*.'

*　　*　　*

236

'We are sorry how things turned out for you, Issy.'

'Thanks Trisha.' I was glad of the sympathy and appreciative when she subtly refused the money I'd offered her for the misappropriated work hours.

'Think of it as redundancy,' she said. 'More importantly, how's the comedy going?'

IT WENT

Within a couple of weeks of my return from Edinburgh, the experience seemed almost mythical and my comedy career to be rapidly dissolving. Geraldine stood true to her word and every club I approached for a gig turned me down. ' 'Fraid there's nothing till after Christmas,' seemed to be the mantra of every comedy promoter, including those who had open-mic spots. So much for my rave review – it was as if Geraldine had issued a blanket embargo on Issy Brodsky. In such a position, ie, with nothing left to lose, I decided to write to Geraldine, to clear my name and offer up the evidence amassed.

Dear Geraldine,
Please find enclosed a video tape. I am sending it without anyone else's interference and in the hope it will clear my name. Lisa may have mentioned she was up for a part in The Parlour, *which, I since heard through the grapevine, she didn't get. This is unfortu-*

nate, as you will notice, should you choose to watch the tape. She really did give her all for it.

Love is such a fragile state to be in and I truly wish that, with respect to yourself and Lisa, I had never become embroiled. Spending time with Lisa, I easily understood how you fell so deeply in love with her. She is a very charming, clever, funny and beautiful young woman. However, from my initial introduction to her it was evident she was not faithful to you (in the physical sense). Geraldine, I have been in the love business a long time and, rightly or wrongly, have reached the conclusion that the truth rarely matters. What happens within a relationship bears no consequence if the expectations of each partner are met, albeit expectations which are very low. Many partners choose to remain oblivious to the antics of their straying loved ones and for most the notion of saving the family precedes acts of infidelity. I realise this is a 'what you don't see won't hurt you' take on life, but on the whole it works, at least on a superficial level.

Geraldine, thank you for the opportunity of a lifetime. I do hope in the future you'll forgive me enough to lift the London comedy club embargo.

Until then . . .

'Well, well, if it isn't . . .'

Yours faithfully,

'. . . the one and only . . .'

Issy Brodsky

*   *   *

Filled with dread, I watched as Fiona rounded the corner into Cecil Sharp House, unsure how the next few moments would play out. Nads's wedding was our second encounter since I'd grappled her to the ground in Edinburgh, bar that phone conversation. As always, she looked fantastic, dressed in Alexander McQueen, and with a rather peculiar-looking man on her arm.

'Fiona's new beau,' Trisha whispered.

Couldn't say he lived up to the word. I suspected that after months of enforced celibacy Fiona went dredging the bottom of the boyfriend barrel. Le Beau was incredibly ugly and not the type of ugly that can become attractive, like Gérard Depardieu or even Woody Allen. This guy was not a visual treat, eyes too close, too deep, nose broken, small. Fiona was at least a foot taller, not including her heels. Standing beside him, Bambuss looked positively gorgeous. I nudged Trisha with my elbow. 'Love is blind.'

She prodded me back. 'Robin Clarke is a super-lovely guy. A total charmer. You'll see.'

They had met on a train. Fiona had been on her way back from the most recent detective convention (location – you got it – top secret, but a long old journey nonetheless). He'd sat opposite her, offered her one of his home-made sandwiches: tinned red salmon, low-fat mayonnaise and heritage tomatoes. She said they were her favourite, how did he know? Had he been at the convention? No, he told her, he was in the relationship business. She couldn't believe it and she revealed she was, too. He opened a packet of salt-and-vinegar crisps, her preferred flavour. They swapped business cards. He ran a matchmaking company, Love Blooms, 'helping relationships to blossom'. The Honey Trap did the opposite, though ensuring 'the sweetest of endings'. Mutually impressed, they chattered on and, when the train pulled into the station, well, let's just say the train pulled into the station.

TAKING THE BULL BY THE HORNS

I guess weddings bring out the best in people and personal animosities can be laid to one side. Fiona marched straight up to me and offered me her hand. I met her halfway, we shook and let bygones be bygones. It all felt very mature.

'You look well, Brodsky.' She smiled, then introduced me to Robin.

'Ahhh!' said Robin.' 'You must be the comedienne Fiona was enthusing about.'

'Guilty.' I raised my hands in jest.

'Fiona says you're very talented.'

'Really?' I was taken aback.

'Told you he's a charmer,' muttered Trisha.

Robin Clarke made up for his physical shortcomings by the largesse of his character. He was obviously doing wonders for Fiona. Love Blooms, Robin informed me, was a dating agency for ladies of a certain age, thirty-recurring being the absolute minimum. 'I'm hoping to persuade Fiona to join forces,' he explained. 'It could be mutually beneficial.'

'What, like, the bad news is your hubby is a philandering jerk, but the good news is there's plenty more fish in the sea.'

'Exactly, Issy. What do you think?'

'Definite potential, very interesting,' I mused. 'Oh, and if you are looking for any new staff . . .'

I donned my *Big Issue* street-seller 'come on, you know it makes sense' grin, only Fiona spotted me. In response she mouthed the letters, 'N. O.' It was then that an usher appeared and asked us to take our seats, so we gathered up our minor responsibilities and shuffled into the grand hall.

Cecil Sharp House was an inspired choice by Nadia, a spectacular space drenched in lovely perfectness and perfectly lovely for a marriage ceremony. The main room was arranged in an informal though intimate way, the hall decked in harvest flowers matching the colours of the huge mural on the wall. As the headquarters of the English Folk Dance and Song Society, its main use was for music, dance rehearsals and performances.

My shoes, though crippling, offered me a fresh perspective and my eyeline met with a sea of necks. Necks beneath hats; hats with feathers, felt hats, delicate hats brought out of the wardrobe only on very special occasions, hats of a purely decorative nature, ie, those that cover neither the ears nor the whole of the crown. I'd never been particularly convinced by objects that were purely aesthetic. Function and beauty was always a far more attractive package, pretty much corresponding with what I looked for in a man.

I was doing the flamingo stance, shifting my balance from one leg to the other, allowing each foot a couple of minutes' respite, disappointed with myself for spending so much money on these instruments of torture binding my feet. At least the dress was a bargain, a knee-length Vivienne Westwood knock-off, although a tad too tight. Max said I looked a bit squashed upfront. 'Squashed but nice, Mum.' Yep, thank the Lord for tummy-tuck knickers: Marks & Spencer's, practical, comfortable, economical, though not especially stylish. I felt safe wrapped inside them, there was a definite womb-like appeal. All those pounds I'd lost in Edinburgh had piled back on the minute I touched down in London. Yeah, all two of them.

Max sat at my side, playing his damned Game Boy (I swear it's a growing boys' pacifier). 'Mum, is it nearly over?' he wondered, sighing, 'I'm bored,' his new catchphrase, before he had even sat down. His boredom threshold was, on average, a ridiculous ten seconds.

'Nearly,' I lied, knowing the service hadn't yet begun.

'When are the band starting?' he asked, though his eyes remained firmly fixed on the small screen in front of him and fingers pressing madly as if engaging in Morse code.

'Soon, I hope,' I empathised. By this time the hall was now comfortably full, late guests arriving at a trickle. It was a patchwork affair, kaleidoscopic in human terms. There was the mixed Caribbean crew of Nadia's family, incorporating African, Asian and even Irish. Tim's family were on one side Anglo Saxon and on the other Nordic, then add in the friends and relatives for a complete pick 'n' mix. The crowd gathered was a perfect illustration of the ethnographical wonder that is London. Acknowledgements were flying, criss-crossing the rows of seats laid out in semicircles.

'How you been, Nora?'

'Look at you, Lionel!'

'When did she die?'

'Wouldn't have recognised you . . .'

A general hush descended and a double bassist began to pluck at his instrument, soon joined by the strings, then a soloist began an acoustic version of 'Milk' by Garbage, sending a collective shudder (in a good sense) down the spines of those gathered. Tim stood at the front of the garlanded podium, his gaze turned to the main door. Accompanied by her children, Nadia slowly and gracefully stepped into the room. Nads's entrance was breathtaking and all of us were transfixed by her staggering beauty. Under a collective gaze, she confidently stepped toward her future husband. From the back there was no way in a million years you would have thought she was pregnant. Her page boy and bridesmaid were deliciously cute standing at her side. I was glad I wasn't chief bridesmaid. It would have looked unbalanced at best, at worst ridiculous.

They had opted for a modern take on a traditional stance, going for the humanistic approach as opposed to religious. The ceremony was led by Fey, a very striking-looking woman in her fifties, with a kind authority in her voice. She spoke about love as an idea and as a reality, the concept of relationships and the expectations of a modern couple. She let us ponder on these conceits as the choir launched into a love compilation, which went from the whimsical to the lovelorn, Tom Waits to The Streets. The effect, I confess, started me off. I could have pretended it was because of my pinched feet or tight dress, or that watching her float into the room, petals strewn at her feet like some '70s disco diva, all soft focus and flaky chocolate, made me realise the decade I grew up in was now retro-chic and, damn it, I was getting on. But really, I was swept up in the emotion of the moment. Okay, I'm a sentimentalist. I was moved. A sophisticated tear delicately wet the sides of my cheeks and I thought how much she deserved this happiness and how lucky I was to have her as a friend.

Uncomfortable with tears making tracks in my make-up, I reached for a Kleenex and, aiming to hold back the flow by forcing darker thoughts to the surface, summoned up 'Lisa'.

*　　*　　*

I have a confession, reader. I did like Lisa, but not in that way . . . well, maybe a bit. I suppose it was like when you're a teenager and you have a girly crush on a goddess prefect. Come on, I am so not the only one this has happened to. To me, Lisa was clever, beautiful, funny, all I aspired to. I almost forgave her that she was a manipulative little shit. She had me sussed early on in the game and knew just how to turn my knobs.

'MUM, I WON PASS THE PARCEL!'

About a week ago I had gone to pick up Max from the first party of the season, Jimmy's sixth birthday at Primrose Hill Community Centre. I tousled Max's hair.

'Have a good time?'

'There was a clown.' Christ, how was I ever going to compete on the party stakes? But as if Max could read my thoughts, he added, 'She wasn't very good.'

Lisa the Clown had been booked for the little uns' entertainment. Dumbing down didn't suit her at all, nor did the brilliant orange and red dungarees. I felt quite embarrassed for her. Packing up her bag of tricks, Lisa clocked me. It was odd, both of us caught out of context, I as a mother and she an idiot.

'Hey, Lisa, never knew you did kids' birthdays.'

'They pay well. It's something you may like to consider. I heard you lost your job.'

'Oh, Issy, can I have a word?' The mother of the birthday boy, busy collecting the party debris, came over. The entire room was awash with half-eaten processed kiddie crap. You know the sort of stuff, a hyper-sugar drink with an additive-friendly cake, and processed cheese of the plastic-strip type plus a pumped-up air roll. It amazes me how people can feed their kids such rubbish. I'd wanted Max to bring a packed lunch. His expression, one of dumbfounded astonishment, told me that perhaps it wasn't a good idea.

I didn't like little Jimmy at all. Unfortunately Max loved him, thought he was the coolest kid ever. I'd seen Jimmy knee a kid in the balls, for no other reason than he could. The kid was Max. I was convinced Jim had a malevolent streak. There's a huge gap between mischievousness (which has a residue of innocence) and knowing maliciousness. Witnessed from my kitchen window, I'd spied the little shit deliberately raise his leg into my son's crotch. Max had begged me to have him over on a play date and then there he was, doubled over, desperately trying to save face. Jimmy reminded me of Lisa. She was a dirty fighter, who pulled low punches when you weren't looking. One arm out to hug you, while the other rammed your stomach lining. Jimmy's mum ignored her son's violent streak, putting it down to high energy.

'Oh, Issy,' she smiled, 'I just want to tell you before Max does that there was a minor incident earlier on. Jimmy got a bit overexcited and pushed Max down the stairs. You know how boys get!' Her head nodded excessively as she spoke. 'Don't worry he's totally fine, no bruises, he was very brave.' She winked. 'We let him win pass the parcel.'

'Why wasn't anyone keeping an eye on them?' I asked flatly.

'Issy, our boys are so raucous, what can I say? Oh there's Saffie's mum. I've got to have word with her. Excuse me . . .'

I turned my attention back to Lisa and in the circumstances couldn't resist a little dig. 'So how's Geraldine?'

'You're so smug, aren't you, Issy?'

'Not particularly.'

'Nice touch with the video.'

'Thanks.'

There had been no response to my letter. Confirmation then, that it had been received and watched.

'You did me a favour.' She smiled with glee, and with her red nose and white, thickly outlined lips appeared somewhat sinister. 'At least my career isn't over, Issy.'

'Oh,' I retaliated. 'Did you not hear . . . ?'

*   *   *

LEGALLY WED AND THERE'S NO GOING BACK

After the ceremony everyone milled about 'ohhing' and 'ahhing' on Nadia's choice of gown, vows and groom, while the official family photos were taken. Then before long a gong clanged, announcing the buffet open and the next stage of the celebrations. I got stuck with cousin Velma who empathised with my blistered feet and revealed her own bunion, looking somewhat like an extra nail-less toe, thus destroying any appetite I'd previously had, which wasn't such a bad thing, considering my dress was cutting into me. Velma recounted her life story, got me to refill her plate twice and then, soon enough, we heard the chiming of a glass, signalling the beginning of the speeches. I grabbed the moment to make my escape and slip away. Hemmed in by her generous figure, I'd gone for an obtuse angled getaway, which meant I was crawling beneath a trestle table, following in Max's footsteps, as it happened. He'd scuttled off ages ago and there I found him with Trisha's youngest, scoffing a large plate of profiteroles, talking Game Boy tactics.

'What are you doing here, Mum?' Max challenged, regarding me with suspicion and embarrassment.

'Don't be cheeky,' I whisper-snapped back and crawled on. It was in this position, while looking for a sizeable exit not blocked by legs, that I heard my name called out. It was Nads making her speech. 'Where *is* Issy . . .?'

Mole-like, my head poked from beneath the table-cloth and up I rose. 'Dropped an earring,' I feebly explained, brushing my dress down, having suddenly found myself in an unexpected spotlight.

'There you are,' Nads continued. 'Issy is one of my best friends, and I wanted to thank her for being there for me during some tough times over the last few years but also to congratulate her on not only having survived the Edinburgh Festival, but recently landed a part in a TV series!'

'Nadia, please, please don't embarrass me.' I was blushing – no, really, I went quite puce.

STAND-UP, ISSY?

At the beginning of the week, I'd received a message on my mobile to call Nell Tony, the comedy agent, which I promptly did.

'Hi, Issy, Nell Tony here, just wondering what your current availability is like?'

'I'm available. Why?' My mind raced. For Nell Tony to call me meant only one thing: opportunity.

'I saw the show in Edinburgh. Thanks for the ticket.'

'Pleasure.'

'Are you going to continue with the stand-up then?' she enquired.

'I'd like to,' I replied. 'I'm just finding it a bit difficult to get a gig at the minute.'

'Yeah, I heard. Issy, I am right in thinking you're a single mother?'

'Yeah . . .' I answered cautiously.

'There's a production company doing a spin-off reality TV show, a mix of *Big Brother, Hell's Kitchen, Wife Swap, Celebrity Love Island*, you get the gist.'

'Yeah?' My intonation was laced with a small degree of wariness, though interested nonetheless.

'They are looking for a group of people from disparate backgrounds, not quite run-of-the-mill folk, they're holding auditions this week.'

'But what exactly is it about?'

'As far as I can make out it's going to be a six-month-long project, documentary-style reality TV. "Contestants" keep video diaries detailing aspects of their lives and at the end of each week viewers vote the most boring off. It could be interesting and would be good exposure. What do you think?'

'Hmm, I'm not sure.'

THE BIG BREAK

Look, it wasn't like I had a job to go back to. The auditions were held in a basement office in Soho. It was a cattle-market scenario, wall-to-wall stars in the making. A form was thrust into my hand and an instant camera in my face. I grinned like a Cheshire, then filled out the questionnaire. Squeezing myself on

250

to the end of a pew, I sat beside an actress in deep conversation with a friend. They were in full scandal flow.

'You'll never believe this.'

My ears pricked up. What could one do but listen in?

'Well?' Lips smacked in anticipation of the juicy rumour.

It involved a certain Casting Agent, no names mentioned for fear of being branded a gossip-monger and thrown off his books (her companion knew exactly who she meant).

'Exactly. Well . . .' This Casting Agent, known for his high brand of sleaziness, ie, couch antics, discovered that one of his 'casting' tapes was (would you believe it?) missing (no!) (yes). He realised he was in deep *merde*. The star of the tape, notorious for being tricky, had already demanded a part and he assumed he was being stitched up by her (professional blackmail), so he got his spoke in first (as it were). Hoping to save his own skin, he grassed her up, spreading rumours of how this actress had fucked him about and shot this illicit tape.

So then what happened?

'Only it wasn't the actress who had the tape, someone else had stolen it and sent it to the actress's girlfriend, that comedy producer . . . What's her name?'

'You don't mean . . .?'

'Exactly, the very one.'

'I don't believe it.'

'Everyone's talking about it. Absolutely everyone.'

NEXT!

I wasn't entirely convinced that qualifying as a contestant on a TV reality show was really where my comedic intentions lay, but seeing as I was an open sort of person . . .

NEXT . . .

. . . thing you know I was offered a part.

'FOR REAL?'

My father thought it somehow cool to use Maxisms.

' 'Fraid so, Dad.'

'Darling,' he jokingly declared to my mother, 'our daughter has finally found her calling!' The pair of them had already shacked up together and were planning a global road trip. It was quite sweet to see them so loved-up, but only in the sickly sense.

'Thanks, Dad.'

'What's that, Issy?' my mother asked, having been handed the receiver.

'Mother, I've been hand-picked out of hundreds of candidates to be, wait for it, one of . . .

'LIFE'S LOSERS'

The band had struck up a good while back with most of us well on our merry way. Trisha and Fiona couldn't restrain themselves from taking the piss out of me, while Max whizzed around high on Coke (of the fizzy kind).

'So, Brodsky, you're going to be a TV star,' Fiona dryly stated. 'One of *Life's Losers*. Has a certain ring to it.'

'Nell, my agent, thinks it will be really good exposure. Millions of people watch these kinds of shows.'

'What, just to see you go about your daily business?' scoffed Trisha.

'Millions . . .' mused Fiona, the implications sinking in.

'And what did your parents have to say?' Trisha coaxed me on.

'Funnily enough, my father's advice was identical to Darren's. He said, "Whatever you do, don't, under any circumstances, give up the day job."'

'What day job, Brodsky?' Trisha laughed.

I looked over to Fiona and mouthed the word, 'Millions . . .'

'Think of all the free advertising,' gasped Fiona. 'Brodsky, you're back on board from Monday.'

SHOWDOWN

Life lands these obstacles in your path and it's up to you to swerve, retreat or stumble forward. Guess I should have watched where I was going, but my mind was full of choice thoughts when we collided in the street, backing into each other.

'What are you doing, Brodsky?'

'Walking backwards, hoping to see where I went wrong in my life, and look where I've stopped.'

'Good to see you, too.'

I was backing into the apartment building as Scarface was on his way out. Chivalrously he helped with my shopping bags and then came into the flat for a coffee. Just a coffee mind, no ulterior motives. Max was delighted to see him. During my absence he'd taken Max out to football on a couple of occasions. Turned out his new girlfriend was one of the Kiwi football trainers. Sure, I experienced a tiny twinge of bitterness, but I was over Scarface, he was too immature for me. I needed someone more, well, just more . . .

His new girlfriend was in her early twenties, malleable, whereas I, it had to be said, was stuck in certain ways and less likely to compromise. In retrospect our incessant bickering had been detrimental to both our senses of self. We'd chipped away at one another. I guess after the hurt abated, there was a latent respect and it seemed we had the foundation of what could be a platonic friendship and, for me, an emergency baby-sitter.

ON COURSE (AND FEELING VERY PLEASED WITH MYSELF)

Fiona and I had patched things up and I'd got my job back, not bad for one of *Life's Losers*, eh? Okay, so we had reached that part of the evening where all of us were hoping for a happy ending.

'So, Brodsky what do you think?' Nads and I were sitting out a love song, feet resting up on facing chairs.

'I think you and Tim have a great life ahead of you.' I raised my umpteenth glass of bubbly.

'You're just saying that to be nice.' We were both tipsified, she rather less so because of her condition.

'Yeah, but I reckon you guys will give it a good go.' Drunkenly I punched the air for effect. 'Cheers, Nads, to you and your new man.'

'Cheers, Brodsky,' and then she chimed in with, 'and here's to you and yours.'

*   *   *

READER!

Look, I didn't want to say anything before, because it was early days, and there was no point in shouting about it from the tree tops, especially if it all went to pot and fell in on itself like Chicken Licken's premonition or one of my soufflés. My favourite dessert, most definitely . . .

MY NUMBER-ONE CHOICE

The gate was closing, the last passengers for the flight called. I heard my name and in that instant put the entire month behind me. My whole Edinburgh experience seemed like a just-played reel of film, the celluloid flapping in its still-spinning can. I rummaged for the ticket in my bag, realised I must have left it at the computer stand and dashed off to retrieve it. I sprinted back to the gate, post post haste and was the last to board the plane. There he was in row thirteen, my number-one choice. My favourite number.

'You're late.'

'Sorry, I couldn't decide what computer game to buy.'

'What did you go for?'

'It was a toss up between Scooby Doo and Super Car Crash Hell.'

'Strange, you don't strike me as a Game Boy addict.'

'It's for my son,' I explained.

'You married?'

'No, how about you?'

'No,' he replied. 'And your choice was?'

'Both, haven't seen my boy in a month, my maternal guilt floweth over.'

'Sounds about right, then.'

'Thanks.'

'Though you are late, and you know how I loathe tardiness.'

'As opposed to tidiness?'

'Plus I wanted the window seat.'

'Well, if you ask nicely I may let you look over my shoulder.'

He said to me, 'Issy, you can be terribly elusive, did you know that?'

To which I replied, 'Thanks, that means a lot.'

'So,' Nadia pressed, 'when are you seeing Jake Vincent again?'

'Tomorrow. He said he was going to show me a mean time.'

'And?'

'We're going to Greenwich.'

Nadia groaned.

'I know, I told him one more quip like that and it's over.'

Greenwich would be our second date, not counting the plane coincidence. On our first date we went for a Japanese and a spot of karaoke. Sake imbibed, we ordered up our song and ended up entertaining a small group of businessmen.

Nadia was eyeballing me. 'And . . . have you kissed?

I nodded.

'And?'

Honestly? It was awkward, our bravado disappeared, it was tender, cautious, took a while to get going and then we ate each other's face off.

'Lovely. And has he met Max?'

I was always very protective of Max in matters of the heart and didn't want to expose him to a conveyor belt of potential daddy/uncles (chance would have been a fine thing!). I adhered to a set of strict regulations, perhaps too rigidly. No potential boyfriend was let through the net (hall door) for at least three months. With Jake, it happened by chance and they met fleetingly at the airport. There we were, flirting away coming out of arrivals and I saw this gorgeous little boy, shouting out my name.

'Mum!' He ran towards me. I scooped him up and lavished kisses on him. I totally forgot Jake Vincent was at my side. In the meantime he'd introduced himself to my mother and gave her his number to give to me.

Nadia was impressed. 'This guy could be the one, Brodsky.'

'We'll see. Come on then, Mrs, time to throw your bouquet.'

*   *   *

FLYING FLOWERS

There was only a handful of eligible women, as most of the guests were in their thirties and already hooked up. I felt fairly conspicuous. It was me, Fiona (which frankly shouldn't have been allowed, considering her new boyfriend), a few teenage girls, various cousins and nieces. Nadia stood about ten feet in front of us with her back to us. We counted down and then she tossed the bouquet over her head. It hurtled mid-centre straight down the line and . . .

RESULT!

Look, what does it matter the girl was only thirteen? She'd have plenty more opportunities and I didn't forcibly grab it off her or indulge in dirty tricks. Her head knocked into my elbow as my arm stretched up to grab the bunch of flowers. That's my story and I'm sticking to it. I slid to my knees, fists clenched, arms pulling down on my victory.

'You're right, Nads!' I hollered. 'This one could be the one.'

The end of an evening and the beginning of a marriage. Goodbyes were issued, carriages were waiting, kisses thrown and then a very tired boy slipped

his hand into mine and away into the night the pair
of us went.

COUNTING ONE'S BLESSINGS

Dear God,
I am on the homeward amble, barefoot and blistered,
thinking over all the stuff that has happened lately. It
doesn't feel too bad being one of Life's Losers. *Know*
what? It feels great. I've my job back, experienced the
Edinburgh Festival, have good friends (oy, reader – get
those fingers out of your throat pronto – I ain't quite
finished), family, a beautiful son, a gorgeous new man.
Not so bad for a thirty-recurring woman.

G, things are boding well, everything's looking up,
so guess that's about it. Oh yeah, before I forget, one
other thing,

Thank you . . . and good night.

A NOTE TO THE AUTHOR

Lana Citron could do better if she beat herself
harder. Easily distracted, she is prone to
daydreaming and should pay more attention
to her grammar.

BY THE SAME AUTHOR

Read the first of Issy Brodsky's adventures in crime,
sex and motherhood in
THE HONEY TRAP.

Ever felt like the world was giving you the finger?

Meet Issy Brodsky, 36–26–36 (in her dreams) agent
provocateur, lone parent of Max and a woman
on a mission. Issy works at the Honey Trap, a
firm specialising in testing men's fidelity. The
Honeys get to play any flirting game they want,
as long as they abide by one rule – never, ever
sleep with a client's husband. Oops . . .

'Funny and vivacious' *Independent*

'An entertaining, sassy crime novel' *Daily Mail*

To buy this book, visit www.bloomsbury.com

A NOTE ON THE TYPE

The text of this book is set in Linotype Sabon,
named after the type founder, Jacques Sabon. It
was designed by Jan Tschichold and jointly
developed by Linotype, Monotype and Stempel,
in response to a need for a typeface to be
available in identical form for mechanical
hot metal composition and hand composition
using foundry type.

Tschichold based his design for Sabon roman on
a font engraved by Garamond, and Sabon italic
on a font by Granjon. It was first used in 1966
and has proved an enduring modern classic.